Cupids Peak

A Holinight Novella

Lee Jacquot

A HOLINIGHT NOVELLA

Cupids Peak

LEE JACQUOT

Cover Design: Cat at TRCdesignsbycat

Edits by McKenzie at NiceGirlNaughtyEdits

Edits & Proofread by Eli & Rosa at My Brother's Editor

A Quick Note From the Author

Cupids Peak is a standalone novella in the Holinights series. None of these books need to be read in order.

It is a steamy & fun read (seriously, it's just a good time) intended for mature audiences of legal adulthood age. It should NOT be used as a guide for kinks or a BDSM relationship.

The author is not liable for any attachments formed to the MCs nor the sudden desire to have someone make you come in places that could get you a ticket.

Reader discretion is advised.

To those who need a feel-good holiday read to fuel their self-care time.

Mia

CHAPTER ONE

"I f you don't get someone to rail you within an inch of your life soon, I'm kicking you out."

My twin sister, Eleni, tosses her phone down on the couch next to me, her lips twisted in a somehow graceful grimace. I've never understood how she's able to do that, but I add it to my mental list of ways she continues to reign supreme in being effortlessly elegant.

"I'm sorry." I pull my pajama-covered legs under me and blow on my hot chocolate, ignoring the soft glow of her phone. "Please explain to me how my having sex has anything to do with my quality as a roommate?"

She brushes her hands over her cream pantsuit. The gorgeous fabric ripples under her touch. "It's like coming home to a sad cat lady with no cats, and it's progressively making your aura suck. You need a good O to bring back some life to those cheeks."

"A good O," I repeat, taking a small sip of my drink and turning back toward my paused Hallmark movie. "I get those every Friday, thank you."

It's the truth, I really do. In fact, I actually have an assortment of toys—all ordered from a discreet shipping site—and rotate them out every Friday while Eleni's on her dates. I'm

1

what some would call a "shy masturbator," and can't seem to find the spot if I know anyone's around to hear.

Eleni throws her hands up before delicately sitting on the leather accent chair next to our couch. "Orgasms should be spontaneous, Em. Not penciled in like something on an agenda."

"Says the woman who goes on dates every Friday," I counter, raising a defiant brow.

Having a solid schedule is one of the few things my sister and I have in common. Everything else, though? Pretty much the complete opposite.

Where she's assertive, I'm reserved. Where she's Miss Fancy-Pants, I'm Miss Cozy-Sundresses. While she's content in front of a dozen cameras being the spokesperson for a multi-billion-dollar corporation, I'm in the background, working on that same corp's finances from the comfort of my couch.

I've never liked being front and center. There's just too much pressure that comes with people watching you, and even imagining them in their underwear does absolutely nothing to help my fried nerves.

"Em, I go out on Fridays because I'm busy during the week, and my Saturdays belong to friends, while my Sundays are for—"

"Errands, I know," I finish for her, taking another swig from my cat mug. And yes, I see the irony. Both in my cup and her telling me to be spontaneous when she herself lives on a tight schedule. "Again, I'll ask. What do my future pet choices and the origin of orgasms have anything to do with you?"

Eleni sucks her teeth, her dark eyes narrowing. "Because our furniture is too expensive to be scratched to hell, and your cunt needs a little love. It helps with your internal balance."

I wave her off, taking another slow drink. I frown when I

notice my whipped cream has already melted. "You're being dramatic, so clearly, there's something brewing. What's up?"

Leaning forward in the chair, my sister crosses her feet at the ankle and rests her hands on her knees. A sly smirk takes over her heart-shaped face. "I got you a date for tonight."

"What?" My brows draw together harshly, the skin pulling taut. "Why the hell would you do that?"

She throws up her hands again. "Because it's Valentine's Day, and you haven't been on a freakin' date in, like, three years."

Annoyance snaps at my rib cage. "Because I've been busting my ass, working close to eighty hours a week."

"Life isn't about working yourself to death, Mia."

"It's not all about having impromptu O's either."

"Then what the hell is it about?" Eleni shakes her head, her dark waves curling around her bronze face. We're both Dominican, but her skin has always been a touch more sun-kissed than mine. *Maybe it's from all her spontaneous orgasms.*

"Look, I'm not asking you to fall in love, but as your sister and best friend, I think you need to live a little, and this is me finally interjecting. Think of it like an intervention or something."

I know my sister's intentions are coming from a good place, and that's the sole reason I don't *accidentally* spill any hot chocolate on her cream pants as I make my way to our kitchen. "And you thought springing this on me the *morning of* would be a great way to do it?"

She snatches her phone from the couch, clearly exasperated that I didn't look at whatever was on the screen. "Of course. It's the only way you'd agree."

That's probably true. Still, I had big plans for today. First, finish my movie, next, stare out of the window at the fresh new layer of snow. Then, maybe take a relaxing bath and watch another movie. It's my day off, so really, the possibilities are limitless. A first date on the love holiday? Definitely not on the agenda.

But also, she's not completely wrong.

My dating life has been, well, for a lack of a better word, dull. The few men I went out with in college weren't looking for anything serious, which I certainly don't blame them for, and the couple after were... not the one.

Hell, now that I think about it, I haven't liked a guy as much as I did this one from my senior year in high school. The funny thing about him was that we never even dated. I'm not even sure if you could define us as real friends. We had random hallway conversations, and then I later tutored him after his math grade threatened to have him benched.

Eli Brooks.

He was the school's *it* guy. Polite, charismatic, with a good sense of humor. A solid trifecta I haven't been able to find since graduating a decade ago. Somewhere in between the late nights and textbooks, I grew really attached to his company. Too bad I couldn't ever muster up my sister's tenacity and tell him.

But even though *we* didn't become something, he did. He's been dubbed the most valuable player on his team in the National Hockey League three years in a row. Not to mention he has somehow become hotter.

Some would say it's a missed opportunity, but I couldn't imagine a worse fate. The man lives in the spotlight. I would have to pop an antacid every twenty minutes.

"I promise you'll have a good time. The guy's a gem and can't wait to have dinner."

I inwardly groan as I re-top my hot chocolate with whipped cream. My sister has good taste in men and an even better radar for the keepers—it's how she actively avoids them on her journey of liberation—so I know she means it when she says he's a catch. Still...

"Who is he?" I finally ask, returning to the couch.

A massive smile overtakes her face. "An old friend of mine from school. He's in town for the weekend, and it just so happens my date canceled on me, but I still have reservations up at Cupid's Peak."

So not a date. A one-night stand.

My eyes widen, and I hold up a hand. "Wait. You want me to go on a date with your old buddy to a *five-star* resort under the premise of him being in town for tonight only?"

She sucks her bottom lips in her mouth and scrunches her nose. "Kinda."

"Kinda?"

Eleni stands. "Listen. If you don't want to go, it's nothing for me to cancel with him. I just thought for once that maybe you'd like to step out of that comfort zone of yours and enjoy yourself."

Enjoy myself. I almost laugh at the direct innuendo. But, per usual, she's right. I could use a night out and maybe have a little fun that's not already pre-penciled in. It would be nice. And with everyone paying attention to their date in front of them, there's no worry about them looking at me.

I bounce my answer back and forth in my mind. Best case, I have a good time. Worst case, it's a night free from having to cook or do dishes.

"Fine."

She lets out a little celebratory *eep* before grabbing her coat on the back of the couch. "I'll let him know. I have a brunch date, but when I get back, we're getting you ready!"

Her words have me on the edge of reconsidering. Eleni getting me ready is the equivalent of a movie-style makeover. One that usually results in her tweezing a couple of random brow hairs and making me wear heels two inches above my max allowance.

But her second excited scream out the front door has me rolling my eyes and shaking my head, returning to my paused romantic comedy. It's stuck on the part where the hero makes the awkward public confession I always have to fast forward through.

I've chalked it up as being the secondhand embarrassment I felt while watching it, but maybe it's the pang of jealousy.

This morning, the news warned of a possible weather system incoming from the north. A downward spike that could bring a little bit of snow, but nothing too bad. As someone who's lived in Colorado her whole life, I know how sometimes the news can be completely wrong.

This is definitely one of those times.

My fingernails dig into the soft padding of my palm as I clench them harder around the rubber handle holding me inside the ski gondola. White flurries slap angrily against the window while the whistle of growing winds seems as loud as an oncoming train.

The storm came out of nowhere and decided to descend on me when I was thirty feet off the ground.

My heart thrums in my chest with every second as the lift ascends up the mountain. I know I'm safe, but if the wind doesn't stop, and they have to stop the gondola... well, I can't think of a worse outcome than some rescue crew coming to get me.

For the next few minutes, I send silent pleas to Mother Nature to get me to the top. I want to take this as a sign that I should have kept my ass on my comfortable couch, but try my best to stay positive. It's hard, though, when my body's swaying with every gust and the chains above are singing their sweet melody of tension. I'm not necessarily terrified of heights, but I'm also not very comfortable with them either.

Almost there. Almost there.

I repeat it over and over until finally, the light of the resort shines through the storm, relieving some of my heart's palpitations. When the lift finally stops and the attendant opens my door, I all but jump out, nearly running into him.

"I'm sorry," I tell him, gripping the side rail.

He shakes his head. "Not a problem. We're actually about to close this until the storm passes."

I start to nod my understanding, but then something concerning grabs hold of my esophagus. "How long until that happens? I'm not an overnight guest."

Going on a first date isn't too bad. Doing it on Valentine's is a little rough. But being stuck at the restaurant? I'd rather stand on stage and sing karaoke. Which is saying a lot.

The attendant shrugs. "They say it should pass within the hour."

Relief slinks through me, only to disappear. The news said we wouldn't be getting slammed with a storm at all, either.

Shit.

Before I follow the path up to the resort, I text my sister about how I've narrowly escaped the icy jaws of death and how she better fly a hot-air balloon to pick me up later if the lifts stay closed. Luckily, though, this is probably the best place to get stranded.

Cupid's Peak is one of the nicest ski resorts in the state. It's been featured on multiple forums since its opening as number one, and I can attest to the absolute beauty of it.

Eleni and I were sent here as part of our company retreat,

and honestly, it's secretly one of the reasons I agreed to the date.

It's as beautiful as I remember. Three stories of floor-to-ceiling glass windows line the front, while twelve floors of immaculate rooms twist around in the shape of a C. Each room comes with a massive balcony, some of which even have hot tubs and fireplaces, while all of them look more like large studio apartments than hotel rooms.

The restaurant is equally impressive, and my stomach growls at the memory of the roasted rack of lamb.

Inside the lobby, warmth envelops me, wrapping around my body like a warm towel after a shower. A shiver runs through me nonetheless as I approach the large oak desk.

The host greets me, her bright red lips curling with a genuine smile. "Good afternoon. So glad you made it safely. Are you checking in?"

I shake my head. "I'm here for a dinner reservation. Last name is de la Cruz."

The woman nods before typing something on the computer. Her eyes search the screen briefly before they widen. "Oh. You're here for—"

She snaps her attention to someone behind me, making me jolt. A gentleman appears from seemingly nowhere and holds out a hand. "May I take your coat?"

My gaze bounces back between the host and him. "Uh, sure." I strip the jacket from my arms and hand it to him. The host's eyes drop the length of my body, and for a moment, a wave of appreciation for my sister's work washes over me. "What were you saying before?"

As the man hands me a coat ticket, a tiny warning in the back of my head is starting to sound. Suddenly, I'm a hell of a lot more nervous than I was a moment ago.

The host shakes her head and comes from around the

counter. "I'll lead you through now. We moved your table to the booths near the back. It's more private and out of direct view of most of the dining area. More romantic, if you will."

My brows squeeze together. "I'm sorry. I'm a little confused. Why did you need to move us?"

The host gives me another smile, but this one is a little more along the lines of "isn't it obvious" before leading me into the attached restaurant. The lights are much dimmer than I remember, and every single table is full. There're couples everywhere, most of which are casually eating, while a few others seem as though they're two seconds away from wanting to suck each other's faces off.

My stomach twists as she takes me around to a row of booths next to the tall glass windows overlooking the slopes. It's an incredible view of the current storm, but it's also extremely intimate and not really meant for a first date. Especially not a blind one.

"Excuse me," I try again. "Can you please tell me—"

"Here we are." The host stops abruptly at the last small U-shaped booth, where a man sits with his back to me. "I'll have your server right over."

I don't even get to thank her before she disappears, but then again, I probably wouldn't be able to. Not when the man has turned around and crushed gray eyes collide with mine.

You've got to be fucking kidding me.

"Hey, Mia. It's been a while."

Mia
CHAPTER TWO

TEN YEARS AGO

"Who do you think Brooks sold his soul to so he could be that perfect?"

My sister nearly chokes on her overpriced water while managing to hack out a still-flattering laugh. "I'm sorry. What?"

Grinning at her dramatics, I take a bite of our mom's left-over pasta and nod toward Eli Brooks. It's lunchtime at school, and I have an unobstructed view of the table he's sitting at. "The devil or a crossroads demon?"

"I—" She lets out a soft snort. "Why in the world do you think he would need to do that?"

I gesture to him again, raising my eyebrows in a "duh" expression.

Eli is sitting with the other hockey players, but really, *they're* sitting with *him*. He's in the center of the long table, an easy smile on his angular face. His sandy brown hair is mussed on top of his head, and his high cheeks are slightly ruddy from fifth-period athletics. But still, he's effortlessly stunning.

All his fellow teammates hang on to his every word, while nearby tables can't help but glance over from time to time, some of them clearly hoping to get his attention.

The best, or in my case, the worst, part about him is how

kind he is. He doesn't let the popularity get to his head, and he's not your typical jock who gets around for the sake of getting around. He's humble, cordial with everyone, and he's funny.

Like *actually* funny, for crying out loud.

As if the gray-eyed anomaly can hear my thoughts, his gaze finds mine, stealing a soft gasp from me. I sit up straighter, but no matter how many times my brain signals for me to look away, my eyes somehow don't receive the message.

I'm stuck in his orbit, completely helpless to the pull of his gravity.

My heart does the cliché double pump, and heat spreads across my cheeks. Definitely wasn't a crossroads demon.

Eleni nudges me on my shoulder. "Earth to Mia."

I blink twice before finally forcing my attention to my sister and away from him. "What?"

She rolls her eyes and takes another long drink. "I was saying I don't think he sold anything. He probably just has awesome parents who did an excellent job raising him."

"We have great parents, but you're still aggressively assertive."

"Ambitious," she counters. "And why don't you ask him after school when you have your little tutoring session?"

I stab my fork through an Alfredo-covered ziti piece a little too hard before shaking my head. "Absolutely not."

"I can find some holy water somewhere. You can just throw it on him casually." Eleni laughs, continuing despite my face being scrunched up in disgust. "You could totally play it off and slip, land into him, and get both of you wet. Just make sure you're wearing a white shirt so that if he doesn't melt, he won't care about the wet clothes."

"You're despicable."

She shrugs, recapping her water. "Maybe a little. But at

least I'm not going to spend a single iota of my life wondering *what if* about anything."

Annoyance slips through me. Why does she always have to be right?

"Because I'm smart," she says, as though she can read my thoughts. Then again, it wouldn't surprise me, being twins and all. "Not necessarily four-point-oh smart like you, but life smart."

I roll my eyes. "You mean street smart."

"Either way, Em, take a chance before you regret it. He's a real catch."

That he is. But even if I did get over the massive lump lodged in my throat when I look at him, I'm not even sure what I'd say. What I'd want.

Being with someone like Eli Brooks would mean life in the spotlight, and that's one of my few hard limits. So what would even be the point?

My eyes flash to the hockey player whose gaze I find still locked on me.

The air thins as he quirks the faintest of smiles and winks.

"Multiplication before division, right?" Eli's smooth voice fills our small booth at my parents' diner.

We come here after school three times a week so I can tutor him for his math class. He likes it because he gets all-you-can-drink chocolate shakes. I like it because it's pretty much my second home. My mom's a waitress and keeps me company while Eleni's at cheer.

"No. But don't stress because that's one of the biggest misconceptions in the math world. It's really whichever operation comes first when reading left to right." I drag a fry through a small mountain of ketchup before popping it into my mouth.

Oddly enough, when we're here in the booth, with just the two of us and no eyes glancing our way, it's easier to be in his presence. More comfortable.

I mean, my nerves still vibrate, and a knot sometimes works its way into my throat when his gaze lingers on me, but it's different from being at school. From when everyone is watching him and paying close attention to who he's talking to. Here, it's like we're in our own little bubble.

"Dammit, that's right. I know this." Eli's light brows furrow and his lips turn down at the corners.

"You do know it. I think you're letting your nerves get in your head because there's a lot on the line."

The whole reason Eli sought me out is because of a recommendation from his math teacher. If he doesn't pass this semester, he won't be playing, and from what I know about him, hockey is his life. It's understandable why he'd get confused under the pressure.

I must admit, though, there's something kind of intimate about seeing Eli get nervous. He usually gives off nothing but easy-going confidence, and I've heard he performs even better on the ice when it's crunch time. Seeing his vulnerable side over the past few weeks has done stupid things to my brain and even dumber things to my heart.

Flipping to another page, I circle a few questions for him to solve. "Do you get this nervous when you're on the ice?"

Eli grunts, sliding his empty glass to the edge of the table. "Never. But that's different. It's what I'm good at. As ridiculous and overused as it sounds, playing hockey is as easy as breathing for me."

I shake my head. "No, I get that. Math is my bread and butter. I barely even choke up around you when I'm talking about math."

What the hell? Why did I just say that?

My chest pulls tight as I wonder where the hell the knot is that usually lodges itself in my throat and prevents me from saying stupid shit.

His steely eyes flash to me, his face unreadable. "Why would you get choked up around me?"

"Because you're Eli Brooks," I say simply, trying to suppress the urge to fidget under the weight of his stare.

He tilts his head slightly, strands of hair falling over his forehead. "And?"

"And," I start, drawing out the word, trying to overlook the way he's gotten somehow sexier in the last four seconds. "You're the most popular guy in school, the top athlete, and subsequently, everyone's crush."

"Sounds like the start of every high school romance movie plot." He smirks before walking his fingers over to my plate. "May I?"

Ignoring the flurry of butterflies making waves in my stomach, I nod. "Yes, and it's a recycled plot because it works."

Before I started tutoring Eli, we'd bonded in the hall over our shared love of eighties movies. Most of them were comedies, but quite a few were romantic.

He shrugs and pops one of my fries into his mouth. "I see. So is this the part of the movie where the jock and his quiet tutor fall for each other? Over shared fries and math problems?"

I'm pretty sure my entire face is on fire at this point as my mind tries to formulate real words. "Uhm—I—no."

Eli laughs, and the sound is enough to soothe all of the anxiety working through me. "I'm messing with you, Mia. I definitely didn't fall for you over math problems."

It takes longer than I want to admit for me to catch on to what he's just said, but when I do, the window to ask him for elaboration has closed. Instead, I discreetly chew on the inside of my bottom lip and stay silent for the next few minutes, watching as he correctly works the set of problems.

Excitement and pride bubble up through my chest, dissolving the lump in my throat. "There you go. You got it."

His eyes round. "All of them?"

"All of them." I hold my index finger out in our celebratory exchange we created one night over our love of aliens in bicycle baskets.

"Fuck yes," he whisper-yells, pressing his finger to mine.

"I'll take that as the session's going good?" My mom appears at the side of our booth, effectively popping our private bubble. "Another shake, Eli?"

He shakes his head, dropping his hand. "No, thank you, Mrs. de la Cruz. I'm actually about to head out."

You are? The thought comes to my mind, but luckily, I'm able to force it back down. I've already messed up once tonight; I don't need to make it a double.

"Did my baby girl get you ready for your final? It's tomorrow, right?"

My eyes flash to my mom and then to him. Finals are already tomorrow? *Shit.*

"Absolutely. I feel great. Thank you again for letting me steal your booth so often."

"It's been a pleasure. Good luck." My mom smiles a goodbye before moving away to help someone else while I'm coming to terms with the fact that this is it. This is our last session, and I'm ninety percent sure he gave me an in, and I messed it up. He probably thinks I'm not even interested.

But I *am* interested.

Shit.

Eli grabs his jacket from the booth and stands, slipping each arm inside.

Say something, Mia.

He pulls his keys from his pocket and twirls them around his middle finger.

Is he hesitating? He's hesitating. Say something.

"Well. Again, Mia, I can't thank you enough for your help." He catches his keys on what appears to be a final twirl and takes a step back.

Shit. Shit. Shit.

I open my mouth, but the wrong words come out. "It's no problem at all. You're going to do great."

One side of his lips twitch, but the slight smile doesn't meet his eyes, and my heart plummets into my stomach, charring in the acid.

"Alright then. I'll see you around?"

I nod, the weight anchoring my extremities into place as he slowly turns on his heel.

Even before he's fully out of the diner's door, I know I'll regret this. I'll regret not trying.

But I'm also not selfish.

He belongs in the spotlight, while the very thought makes me viscerally ill. He needs to be with someone that matches those needs, and I am not that person.

At least, that's what I tell myself to make the feeling in my chest ache a little less.

Eli

CHAPTER THREE

Ten years ago, I was dumb enough to let Mia de la Cruz slip through my fingers.

I knew her quiet and reserved nature was the opposite of mine and what I had in store for my life, and I figured it would be best for *her* to be the one to make the first move. That way, I'd know without a doubt she wanted me despite it.

My intentions were there, but the execution wasn't, which is why I finished high school having to admire my girl from a distance. I watched her kill it at the top percent of our class and give an inspiring, heartfelt speech during our graduation.

She'd struggled to start at first. Her eyes were darting around, her hands fisting the edge of her gown while she shifted from foot to foot. But then, out of nowhere, those brown eyes landed on me, and she started speaking as if it was just her and I in the whole damn stadium.

It rekindled my hope that maybe we could try to be something regardless of our obvious differences. But when I went to find her after the ceremony, I overheard her with her sister and learned it wasn't me she was looking at, but Eleni, who was sitting right behind me.

I'd thought when I graduated and went off halfway across

the country for college, I would forget about her. That those few weeks we spent together would be a distant memory belonging to a time everyone usually tries to forget.

But I didn't, not entirely. Every once in a while, I would do something or see something that would remind me of her. It could be as obscure as eating out and sitting in a booth or as direct as drinking a chocolate shake. The moments would be fleeting, but her smile, her laugh, would fill me with a homey feeling I can only describe as the one you get when you watch something from your childhood.

After graduating, I got picked up by my current team in the NHL and I sort of cherished those random moments even more. It sated my homesick heart until the off-season when I was able to go back.

Luckily, we played in town last night, and I happened to run into Eleni, Mia's sister, the next morning on my way to get breakfast. She was a socialite in high school, and we ran with a lot of the same people and would often end up at parties together. We decided to catch up over a coffee, and by the end, she was telling me to take her reservation at Cupid's Peak and to go with Mia. Knowing Eleni for as long as I have, there's no arguing with that woman—even though I had no intention of doing so—and I agreed to the date.

I won't lie and say I haven't been nervous as hell. In fact, it's all I've been. Part of me was worried that I'd been using her as this good feeling for so long that when I actually saw her, it wouldn't be the same. That I let her memory turn into something so great in my mind that it would no longer be realistic.

But the moment my eyes meet her big brown ones, I realize how much of an asshole I've been. How nothing I've imagined or remembered has held a candle to the real thing.

She's fucking gorgeous. Her long brown curls are twisted away from her delicate face, falling over exposed shoulders.

Her outfit's thin straps lead down to a soft pink dress that shows a teasing amount of tan cleavage and flares at hips my fingers itch to hold.

My sternum tightens as I stand, staying in the hidden shadows of the dim booth. I lift one arm, and she leans into me, wrapping an arm lightly around my back. The touch innocent in nature, but the way her fingertips curl slightly into the side of my rib cage makes my pulse thrum even harder.

"Eli, what a surprise. How are you?" Her voice is slightly high, and I appreciate that I'm not the only one nervous.

"I'm doing alright, Mia. How about yourself?" I reluctantly release her, allowing her to sit.

She nods to the window. "I had both an adventure and a near-death experience coming up, but I'm good now."

I chuckle. "I'm grateful it was only near death."

"Same." She smiles, her dimples peeking through and reminding me how much I've missed seeing them. "I can't believe Eleni didn't tell me *you* were the blind date. I definitely wouldn't have given her such a hard time."

I quirk a brow, trying to ignore the pride blooming in my chest at her comment. "Oh yeah?"

"Of course. I—" She pauses, almost as if to think better of what she's saying, then shakes her head. "Seeing an old classmate is a relief. Especially you. Now, tell me how you've been."

Before I can respond, a server greets us. It's clear the manager gave her the usual privacy spiel that accompanies me everywhere I go because her voice is more hushed than necessary. Though, when her gaze lands on me, it's clear the "no-gawking" part was skimmed over. "Hello, my name is Veronika. Can I start you off with a glass of our house wine?"

My eyes flash to Mia, whose lips curl in a polite smile. "Just a tea for me, please."

Veronika's brows furrow in the middle, as though Mia

asking for a warm drink in the middle of a blizzard is outrageous. After another beat, she gives her a curt nod and turns to me, an absurdly large smile on her face. "Um, yes, of course. And for you, sir?"

"You wouldn't happen to have chocolate shakes, would you?"

Mia covers her mouth, doing a horrible job of hiding a laugh, while the server looks genuinely bewildered.

Veronika passes a look between Mia and me before clearing her throat. "For you, I'm sure I can work something out. Did you want to start with any appetizers? We have our Oyster Rockefeller, avocado bruschetta, or perhaps our cucumber shrimp?"

"Anything sound good to you, Mia?"

She shrugs. "The bruschetta?"

I nod, not taking my eyes off hers. "We'll have that, please."

The server smiles at me again, her eyes lingering in my periphery long enough to draw Mia's attention, but I don't turn and instead focus on Mia. "Tell me, what have you been up to?"

She purses her lips, pulls them from side to side as she waits for Veronika to leave, then sighs. "Nothing, really. I mean, I went to college and started interning at a communications corporation with my sister. Then graduated and moved to their finance department. I work from home, which means I spend way too much time in pajamas and am pretty sure I've cleared my Hallmark movie backlist."

This gets a laugh from me. "Impressive. Do you have a favorite trope, or is it still the tutoring one?"

Mia's eyes widen slightly before she grins. "It's still a top five for me. But I think city girl gets amnesia and has to work on a farm, and CEO who needs a fake fiancée, are fighting for the top spot."

21

"Ah, the good old amnesia one. You're right." I lean forward, resting my forearms against the table. "That's top-tier stuff right there."

Her brown orbs roll playfully. "Okay, but seriously, your life seems way more exciting. Tell me what it's like kicking ass on the ice."

My brows lift. "You watch me play?"

She shrugs. "Maybe once or twice."

Satisfaction swells behind my ribcage. Even if it was only once, I like that she's thought of me after high school. "Well, thanks to you, I passed Mr. Clorey's class and played my best season yet. I got a full ride over in Minnesota and was drafted for my current professional team."

Mia beams. "I knew you were going to pass that class. Speaking of which, I saw Mr. Clorey the other day."

"Oh yeah? Is he still a dick?"

"He was quizzing a random ten-year-old about how much it would cost him to buy two pounds of organic bananas versus regular ones."

I chuckle. "Sounds about right."

The server returns with two glasses of water, a cup of tea, and my miracle of a chocolate shake. It's in a low tumbler glass, and two cherries rest on the side, stabbed through a cocktail pick.

"I'll be back in a moment with your bruschetta. Is there anything I can get you in the meantime?"

"No, thank you, Veronika." I shake my head, plucking the pick from my milkshake and holding it out to Mia. "You still like the cherries, right?"

"You remember that?" She scooches over the U-shaped booth slightly, taking the stick from me and putting it on her napkin.

"How can I forget when you stole every single one of mine?"

Her mouth drops open. "I would never! Do you know how nervous I used to be when we'd get together?"

"No, you weren't. Not the way you used to be on my ass about getting the Order of Operations wrong."

Mia scoffs. "I was the nicest tutor."

I shrug. "Debatable."

She tilts her head back with the laughter I also didn't quite remember right. It's light and infectious, spreading through me and making everyone else in the damn restaurant disappear. "Says the *nice* guy who gets put in the penalty box once every game."

"So you've seen more than one game," I point out, trying a bit of the chocolate shake. It's more nostalgic than it is good, and it sends me to a place with little of life's troubles. "Your mom's shakes are way better."

"Yeah, I'm sure. Some things are better left to mom-and-pop restaurants."

I wash the thick chocolate milk down with some of the water. "I see how you skipped over that part about watching my games."

Mia hides her smile behind her mug as she takes a sip that takes way too long, buying herself time before she has to admit she's thought of me a little more than once or twice. But of course, she's saved by Veronika, who appears with our avocado bruschetta.

She's quick to take our orders, but when she turns to leave, Mia stands, asking for the ladies' room.

When she walks away, I try my fucking hardest not to watch, but my eyes don't seem to care and follow the curves of her frame all the way through the sea of tables.

My blood rushes through my veins, a vision invading my

thoughts of having her come undone at the table with people just a few feet away. How she'd have to muffle her moans and hide the orgasm ripping through her as nearby couples enjoyed their Costolette Brasato.

The thought is sudden and reminds me why this didn't work back then and why it definitely wouldn't work now. Mia has always been the type to stay out of everyone's line of sight. She likes keeping to herself and probably prefers her orgasms to be inside, in her bed, hidden in the dark.

My life in the light has done nothing but move into a bigger ray, and my desires in bed are pretty much the same.

All this time and I doubt our story would ever change. She'll simply remain a sweet dream, just out of reach.

Mia
CHAPTER FOUR

"I 'm literally going to strangle you. Eli Brooks?" I push my mouth closer to the receiver of the phone, making my whisper sound more like an incoherent hiss. "Eli *fucking* Brooks, Eleni? What were you thinking?"

I snuck off to the bathroom to call my sister. The restrooms here are fancy as hell, and I'm in one of those stalls that's its own private room. My palms are slick, my stomach doesn't know if it wants to sink or float away, and I have goose bumps that I'm pretty sure are permanent at this point.

When I tutored him in school, there was work to do, something to keep my mind off the fact I was a foot away from him in a pretty intimate setting. Now? It's me, him, and an already established one-night expectation.

"I'm thinking you need to get laid, and what better way to do it than with someone you used to know and have a crush on?" Her voice is borderline sing-songy, and I envision myself giving her a noogie like when we were younger. She used to hate it when I messed up her hair, but the second of imperfection was enough to get me out of whatever misery she was putting me through. "Think of it as marking something off your bucket list."

An odd combination of annoyance and gratitude swirls together in my gut, forcing a sigh from deep in my chest. "*Had* a crush. And having a one-night stand with a celebrity hockey player is not on my Bingo card."

"Bucket list. And *had,* my ass. I know you have that dumb sports channel programmed on the clicker." Glasses clink together in the background, and the faint sound of lofi can be heard somewhere behind her. "Also, I threw you my phone. It had his damn picture on it."

I internally groan at myself for not taking the two seconds to look down this morning. But then again, I probably would have talked myself out of coming because of nerves. I did have the biggest crush on him and completely fumbled it.

Honestly, though, it's probably for the best. I wanted as far from the world's eye and scrutiny as possible, and the man literally lives under a microscope.

My sister releases a long breath. "Em, please go out there and have a good time. Take a couple of shots, make out, and please, for the love of everything, fuck that man in the gondola on the way down."

"Eleni!"

She laughs. "I'm serious. Live a little, girl. It's one night. No more what-ifs."

No more what-ifs.

I've been lucky enough to not have many, but Eli has always been my biggest one. Do I owe it to myself to have a non-battery-powered orgasm? Yeah, sure. Do I owe it to my smitten teenage self to do just that with Eli Brooks? Definitely. But to fornicate on a lift where anyone could see us?

That's definitely going to take something a lot stronger than my current drink of choice. "Fine, but no promises on the PDA."

I can feel my sister's smile through the phone. "Go big or go home, Mia."

Shaking my head, I hang up and exit the stall. A girl who's two sinks down from me is on the phone as she applies her red lip. "No, I swear it's him. Malik's gonna see if he can get an autograph."

This is the part where I'm supposed to be like "see, he's too well-known," or maybe irritated random strangers are comfortable interrupting my date on Valentine's, but instead, I feel... pride. Excitement.

Out of all the people in the world someone like Eli could be spending his Valentine's with, he's spending it with me. With his reputation and notoriety, it's likely we'll be seen together and possibly even photographed and put in some tabloids.

And he's okay with it.

Talk about an ego boost.

After washing my hands, I make my way back through the restaurant, where I find Eli doing what looks similar to a fist bump to a man with red hair. When they move their hands, I realize their index fingers are pointed—something I've seen him do with other teammates after a goal.

"Am I interrupting?" I smile, retaking my seat at the booth.

"I'm sorry," the man starts. "I saw a moment he was free and couldn't help but come say hello. I'm a huge fan of your boyfriend."

Eli shakes his head. "Not a problem. It's always a pleasure to meet a fan."

The man shakes Eli's hand before going back to his table. When he's far enough that he can't overhear, I ask the obvious, "I'm not sure what I should be more curious about. The fact I have a famous boyfriend I knew nothing about, or if it bothers you to be recognized everywhere you go."

One corner of Eli's lips lifts, and my core clenches in response. It's hard looking at him and not considering my sister's words.

His angular jaw is now covered in a short, neat beard. A few faded scars that I find unreasonably sexy decorate his slightly crooked nose, temple, and left cheek. All of them courtesy of tussles on the ice, and all of which I watched through tiny slits in my fingers that covered my eyes. His body has filled out as well. Lean muscle has turned into bulk mass, his white button-down fitting a little snug across his shoulders and arms, displaying the strength required to fight off angry opponents.

The years have done him justice.

"I apologize about that. Sometimes it's easier to go along with people's assumptions." He leans into the booth, propping his arm along the back. "And no. I'm used to it now. There's actually a kind of motivation that comes with always having people watching you."

"Motivation? More like irritable bowels."

Eli chuckles. It's low and sensual and sounds like something I'd very much love to hear in the crook of my neck. Or running down my side. Or between my thighs.

My face heats at the vision trying to invade my mind. *Holy shit.* I need to get myself together. I'm letting my sister get into my head.

Clearing my throat, I push the thoughts away. "What do you mean, motivation?"

His hand closes around his glass of water on the table, thumb moving up and down slowly, disrupting the drips of condensation. The act itself is innocent enough, but it incinerates the weak hold I have on my raging horniness.

"Knowing people are watching me..." He pauses, his low gaze flicking up to mine. His gray irises have my heart pounding faster and my breath coming a little quicker. "It encourages me to do more. Do better."

My bottom lip disappears between my teeth as I try to capture some type of coherent speech. "I—um, I can understand that."

He arches a brow. "Can you? You were always so nervous in front of people when we were in school."

"Oh, I still am. My skin gets hot, my tongue feels thick, words are harder to grasp. Whole nine yards. But I completely get how it can act as an external motivator too."

His head moves up and down slowly in understanding. "When's the last time you were in front of a large group of people?"

My answer is instant because I still have nightmares about it. "Graduation."

"Oh wow, that long ago?"

I nod. "Yep. Even the interview for my job was with a small panel of three people, and it was over a video conference."

Eli glides a large hand through his hair, the muscles in his biceps flexing through the fabric. "I remember that speech. You did really well."

Internally cringing, I shake my head. He's being kind. "Well" is the perfect *antonym* for how I was up there. I still can't believe I let my family talk me into it in the first place. "When I say I barely made it through without puking on everyone in the first row, I mean barely."

He chuckles, the sound twisting with his smooth voice. "I mean, at first, yes. You looked a little like a deer in headlights. But once you locked eyes with your sister, it was great. I was proud of you."

"My sister?" My head tilts to the side slightly. "I was so frazzled, I couldn't even find her in the arena."

Now it's his turn to look confused. His mouth parts twice, and a deep valley forms between his brows. "She sat right behind me. You stared at her the entire time."

I'm not sure what's funnier. Him thinking I could see anyone behind his large frame or him believing I *wanted* to see anyone else besides him.

Maybe it's my sister screaming in the back of my head or the reality that I really don't want to leave this dinner with any regrets, but I tell him the truth. "I was staring at you, Eli."

He narrows his eyes in suspicion. "No way. I saw you after the ceremony. Your sister was saying she was glad you were able to focus on your happy place."

A vicious heat blooms across my cheeks. Okay, maybe I didn't want to be *that* honest. Luckily, the waitress appears with our food and grunts disapprovingly in my direction when she eyes the nearly full appetizer plate.

"Is there anything else I can get for you?" It's clear her question is more for Eli than the both of us, and with the way she's been openly gawking at him, I'm sure the question is loaded. Can't say I blame her, though.

"Can I have a mojito?" I know one drink won't do anything, but I need the placebo of liquid courage if I have any hope of saying "fuck it" and taking a risk with this man.

Eli's eyes snap in my direction, making my pulse stutter. I manage a soft smile, which he returns, and I'm pretty sure my panties are now disturbingly wet.

His gaze slowly drags away from me and finds Veronika's. "Two of those, please."

"Coming right up, sir." Like before, she lingers a few extra seconds before disappearing back through the cluster of tables.

"This looks really good." I pick up my fork, hoping to redirect the conversation, but Eli shakes his head.

"Uh-huh. No way. What's the happy place thing about?"

"No chance of dropping it?"

He shakes his head. "Not one."

Rolling my eyes, I give in. "I'll tell you, but I need your word that you're not going to judge me."

Eli holds up three fingers. "Scout's honor."

A nervous shiver runs through me as I explain how my happy place has always been the diner. My mom and dad opened it before we were born, and I loved being there all the time. Even though it was usually full of people, I still had my slice of peace in the midst of it all. Those weeks that Eli and I worked together made me realize a few things, the main one being that the booth wasn't the only thing that could calm my nerves.

He could too.

I'm still not sure what it was about him, but even though I still experienced my typical shyness, I always felt safe. Unjudged. Free to be me.

So when I was giving my speech, and I found him in the crowd, I imagined it was just him and I, back in my parents' diner, sitting in our corner booth.

Eli eats his food in silence as I ramble on, and when I'm done, I'm a little winded and confident my heart has left a bruise on my ribcage.

When he continues to not say anything for a minute, anxiety starts to squeeze my insides. Doubt seeps in as well, tugging on my heart. *Why did I—*

"Will you play a game with me, Mia?"

Somehow, I'm able to keep the shocked laughter in check. "A game?"

He nods.

I start to open my mouth to ask a question but decide against it when none come to mind. I basically just told this man he was a cure for my social anxiety, and he's asking me to play a game.

Some of the withheld laughter seeps out. "Um, sure. What game did you have in mind, Mr. Brooks?"

A smirk that looks like something the devil would wear before sealing a deal slips across his face. "Truth or dare."

Mia

CHAPTER FIVE

I'm currently sitting in a booth at a five-star resort with Eli Brooks, my old high school crush and current star of a leading hockey team, about to play a game of truth or dare. I'm not sure where I thought my night might lead, but it definitely didn't involve this.

"I'll let you go first," Eli says, taking a bite out of his broccolini. His jaw flexes as he chews, and there's something about his working throat that does wicked things to my imagination. "And I'll pick truth."

Truth. Ha. My truth right now is that I'm very quickly taking on a whole new persona. How I feel like now I could very easily scoot around the U-shaped booth and close the increasingly annoying gap between us, despite the number of eyes that have slowly begun shifting in our direction.

There's always been something about being with Eli that eased the nerves of being around others. I'm not sure if it's his general, easy-going personality, those damn eyes of his that lasso me in and refuse to let go, or just how nice he is to look at. But right now, it's encased us in a little bubble, similar to how it did back in high school. There's only him and me, and a little game I intend to use to give myself some closure. Of knowing what I felt back then wasn't one-sided.

I pick up my cocktail and nearly down the whole thing in two gulps.

Let's do this. "When's the last time you've been on a date?"

He takes a slow drink of his mojito and smirks behind the rim. "Does our time in the diner count? Because if so, ten years ago."

I scoff, unsuccessfully tampering down the influx of excitement threading through me. "The game is called *truth* or dare, Eli. Not say cute things you think'll help get you under my dress."

As soon as the words come out, my eyes snap open and my hand flies over my mouth. I can feel the heat of embarrassment flush over my face and suddenly it seems as if there's a dozen more eyes looking our way.

I understand the parameters surrounding this date were initially a one-night thing for me, but I can't be certain it had the same meaning for him. "I'm sorry, that was really forward. I don't—"

Eli waves me off, relaxing more in the booth. "No, I get it. The general consensus is that people say things they know will get them laid."

A wave of appreciation for him not giving me a hard time washes over me. I chew on the inside of my lip. "I doubt you have to say anything at all. You probably get more attention than you know what to do with, just like in high school."

On a few occasions, Eli would have to shut off his phone during our tutoring sessions. It would vibrate in his bag at least four to five times every couple of minutes, and I could tell it was sometimes too much.

One of his shoulders lifts half-heartedly. "The only attention I ever wanted, I'm getting right now."

My eyes flash to him, but my throat is suddenly so thick all I can do is stare. So maybe it wasn't so one-sided after all.

Elation works its way through me, my body warming at the notion.

He huffs out a small chuckle, stabbing his fork through another tender green. "And just so you know, it wasn't a lie. I've been, what some would say, a little too busy to date. And to the latter, I have no intention of saying anything *cute* to get in between your thighs."

Even though I'm sure his words are meant as another way to calm my nerves, it only ramps them up more. They could mean a million different things, and with the way my pussy clenches, demanding to know exactly what he means, I can't stop myself from figuring it out. "More of a dirty talker, are we?"

Oh my god, Mia. Shut up! That was definitely not what I meant to say.

I grab one of the bruschetta pieces from the corner of my plate and take an obscenely large bite. It's an attempt to keep my mouth busy from saying something else completely mortifying while also hiding the vicious blush burning across my face.

But instead of responding at all, Eli tilts his head slightly, letting those gray orbs roam over me slowly.

I feel the heat of his eyes as they touch every part of me.

My lips.

Across my jaw.

Down my neck.

Over my collarbone.

Goose bumps prickle along my skin and the moment his gaze finds mine again, I'm all but panting. I don't remember Eli ever being this... *intense.* The boy version of him tugged on every soft part of me, threatening to steal my heart with the wink of his eye. But this Eli—the man he's become—is promising to *own* every part of me, and that is equally erotic and terrifying as hell.

"You could say I'm direct," he finally says. "I like to say what I want, how I want it, and how they're going to give it to me."

Fire immediately erupts deep in my core. *Fuck me.*

I worry at my bottom lip and readjust in the booth. My clit is now throbbing, and tightening my thighs does nothing to relieve the sudden influx of pressure. Still, I manage to find my voice, needing to know without a doubt how he feels. "And what is it that you want, Eli?"

"Hmm. But it's my turn now, Mia. Truth or dare?"

The temptation to demand an answer is strong, but I push it down. "I just told you all of my truths, an embarrassing amount, in fact, so I think I'll pick dare."

His brows lift. "Are you sure?"

His tone is somewhere between a warning and a challenge. Excitement and trepidation take hold of me, and for a second, I consider changing my mind.

We're in a restaurant full of people—over half of which know who he is—what could he really even dare me to do?

I nod, taking a bite of my lamb. It's as tender as I remember, breaking apart and nearly melting on my tongue. "Do your worst."

One corner of his lips hitches up. "I dare you to come over here."

"What?"

He sets down his fork and uses his index finger as he speaks. "I want you to take your plate, and move over here on this side of me."

My gaze focuses on where he's pointing on the left side of him.

The booths are small, intimate, semi-circles. The backs are

fairly average height, reaching to Eli's shoulders, and they butt up to the seamless wall of glass overlooking the slopes. If I move around, people will only be able to see Eli.

I vaguely wonder if it's purposeful because of the attention that's drifted our way since that person greeted Eli. It would take me out of the general view and put me closer to him. Win-win, really.

"Would you like to switch?" he asks, a playful smile teasing the edge of his mouth.

"Not at all." I move my water first and then my plate before sliding around, stopping about six inches away from him.

Being this close to him, I can make out the warm earthy scent of his cologne and feel the pure heat radiating off his body. My nerves ignite, my muscles tense, and no matter how much I attempt to channel my inner confidence, I can't drag my eyes up to meet his.

"Comfortable?"

"Yes." My voice is a lot breathier than I want it to be.

"Then why is your body so stiff?"

A humorless laugh shakes my body. "I'm a tense person."

He *"hmms"* before returning to his food. Thankfully, I'm left-handed, so the close proximity doesn't make eating awkward.

"So it's your turn. Truth or dare?"

He doesn't even think about it. "Truth."

Normally, I'd tease him about taking the easy choice, but then again, I wouldn't even know what to ask if he picked dare. "This might sound a little strange, and you probably won't even remember, but there was something you said when I was tutoring you, and it stuck with me for a while. I always regretted not asking you what you meant."

Eli's lips draw down, and he shifts to look at me. "I'm intrigued."

A sigh works from my chest as I gear up for what could be nothing.

Or it could be everything.

"You mentioned not falling for me while I taught you math. What exactly did you mean?"

I sometimes wondered if he meant he could never like someone like me, or if he already did, and it wasn't because I helped him pass Mr. Clorey's class.

"Oh. That one's easy. But you have to promise you won't get mad."

Now it's my turn to be intrigued. I hold up my index finger toward him, an unspoken agreement to the promise. I wonder if he even remembers our little gesture. It was something like a secret handshake, inspired by our love of movies made in the seventies and eighties.

We figured out that little tidbit our sophomore year when he was wearing a high school shirt from the Ferris Bueller movie on the same day I was wearing a shirt with ET on it. We ended up talking in the hallway until we were both late, and he stuck his finger out for me to touch.

We became "passing acquaintances" after that. Sometimes striking up conversations about movies during our passing period and giving trivia every once in a while to see who knew them better. When we left for class, we always touched our index fingers.

Eli smiles before resting his fork at the edge of his plate and connecting our fingers. When he drops his hand, he pushes out a breath and starts, "I've had a thing for you since freshman year when I overheard you and your sister talking about who you'd fuck-marry-kill when it came to the cast of *The Breakfast Club*."

I don't hold in my laughter, and when I snort, I laugh harder. "You're lying."

He shakes his head. "No, I'm dead serious. When you told her you'd fuck Richard? I almost dropped to one knee."

"I only said it because it drove Eleni crazy. She couldn't wrap her head around it."

Eli nods. "Oh, I know, and it was funny as hell to watch her try and all you said was—"

"Age gap is a thing. Don't shame me," I finish, remembering that conversation as clear as day. "I can't believe *that* made you interested in me."

He leans in slightly, drawing one hand up slowly as his eyes rove over my face. The laughter dries in my throat when the side of his hand brushes against my cheek. I wait, my breath stalled in my lungs, as he tucks a hair behind my ear.

"It was one of many."

My voice doesn't return until he drops his hand, moving to grab his fork. "And why would I be mad at you for that?"

He pauses for a second, swinging his utensil back and forth as though he's unsure what to eat. Or maybe it's that he's searching for the right words. Finally, he peers up. "Because I didn't really need a tutor for math."

My brows furrow. "Wait. What?"

At the same moment his lips part, a gust of wind slaps a flurry of snow into the window behind us. It's been steadily flowing since we sat down, acting as beautiful scenery to add to the dark ambiance inside, but now I realize how hard it's coming down.

Like, if it doesn't ease up soon, we won't be leaving, coming down.

Anxiety swirls around in my chest, threatening to steal the swell of arousal he's inflicted. We can't stay here. It's Valentine's Day, and this resort is notorious for being booked months out.

For the first time, I'm actually happy to see our server

appear at our table. Her eyebrows snap together, creating a deep valley between them. I assume she's curious as to our new seating arrangement but doesn't say anything. Instead, she corrects her facial expression and smiles at Eli. "I hope you're finding everything to your liking."

"We are," Eli replies, still studying my face.

Veronika clears her throat, shifting on her feet. "Very good. Well, the hotelier has informed us that the storm is projected to worsen and highly advises all guests to stay until it's passed."

"We aren't overnight guests," I inform her, my body becoming even tenser.

Veronika nods. "Yes, well, as luck would have it, there is one room available as a couple wasn't able to make it here before the storm."

Eli finally glances at her. "We'll take the room."

Our server looks slightly star-struck as he gives her his full attention. I know the feeling all too well, and again, can't even get mad at her obvious attraction. "Yes, sir."

She leaves us alone again, and then he returns to his meal as if he didn't just drop a nice little bombshell, complete with an overnight decision. "Okay, I need to know what the tutoring thing is. What do you mean you didn't need it?"

"It's my turn, though, love. Truth or dare?"

My lips part, my heart palpitating at how easily a term of endearment fell from his mouth. At how much I like it.

"Um—dare."

A smirk breaks across his face, and I know I'm a goner before he even says the words. "I dare you to let me show you how obsessed I was with you ten years ago."

Mia

CHAPTER SIX

How obsessed I was with you ten years ago.

Eli's gray eyes sweep over my face before he turns nonchalantly and resumes eating as though he hasn't tilted me on my axis.

I crushed on this man for damn near three years and he lowkey felt the same?

Irritation grips my stomach, turning it over. I loathe watching movies with the miscommunication trope, and I'm currently being shown just how easy it is to fall into its snare.

"Why didn't you say anything?" I ask, stabbing my fork a little too hard through a grilled carrot.

Eli lifts one shoulder. "Honestly, I was nervous."

I scoff. "You, nervous? Come on, Eli. Not only were you a really popular guy, but you starred on the hockey team and could get any person attracted to the male species. Why the hell would you be nervous?"

"Fear of rejection is a thing," he says simply. "Besides our mutual appreciation for eighties cinema, we were pretty much opposites."

"And?"

"And—" He reaches for his rum, taking a large swig before

turning toward me. "I didn't think someone like you would bother with me."

I let out a bitter laugh, scooting back slightly so I can fully face him. "Who is someone like me?"

He tilts his head, his lips tugging at one side. "Someone who will literally volunteer to pull their teeth out and then swallow them like clonazepam rather than participate in anything in a public setting."

My mouth drops open as he recites word for word what I told my communication group when one of them asked if I would give our presentation my junior year. As a matter of fact, now that I think about it, it was one of Eli's teammates who suggested I do it. When he did, the whole group looked at him as if he'd grown a second head. My preference to be a support in the background has never been a secret.

"I'm a social person, and I never had any intentions of pursuing you if I knew you'd be miserable with me. I wanted to know if you could, or would, ever leave your comfort zone, so I asked a friend to see if you'd give your group's speech."

Something foreign pinches in my chest. I'm not really sure how to articulate the feeling, but it's somewhere between admiration that he didn't want either of us to waste time pursuing something we'd inevitably hate, or angry he didn't try.

"So why agree to this date tonight?" My voice comes out a little harsher than I mean it to be. "Did you think I changed?"

Despite my snippy tone, Eli shakes his head slowly. "Not at all. I wanted to see you. Catch up."

A dark suspicion creeps up from nowhere and injects me with its venom. It spreads through me, putting together puzzle pieces I hadn't even considered until now. My sister made it clear he was in town for the weekend, and this is a one-night thing. He also said he hasn't been on any dates because he's been busy.

My *aha* moment is equally dawning and painful. "It had nothing to do with the fact that I'm the perfect candidate for a one-night stand, who won't post all over social media how she slept with the infamous Eli Brooks?"

Saying it feels a little childish, but it makes sense in my head.

Eli laughs. It's deep and robust, and *holy fuck,* even though I'm kind of pissed, it's sexy as hell. "Do you want me to stand up in the middle of this restaurant and let everyone know I'm here with you? I'll do that, pay, and go home. Then I'll lay on my stomach and FaceTime you so we can talk until the sun comes up."

I suck my lips in to keep from laughing, but then he abruptly stands, yanking my heart into my throat.

My hand reaches up and not so softly jerks him back toward his seat. "Don't you dare."

He doesn't entertain my weak grasp but gazes down at me. "Why? Don't want the world to see me on the most romantic day of the year with my great white buffalo? That even after all these years, I haven't found anyone who makes me smile or laugh or feel at home the way you did?"

My heart squeezes. It's funny how when I watch my movies, I think of these moments as the most cringe-worthy material and often wonder who would actually like confessions like this.

But it's me. I very much like hearing him say I'm the one that got away. In fact, I want a little more context. "Ah, so *this* is what you say to get in between my legs."

It's meant to be a joke—at least, kind of—but Eli sits down and leans forward, gripping my chin lightly with his thumb and forefinger, stalling the breath in my lungs. "I had no intentions of coming here just to fuck you. Do I want to? Abso-fuckinglutely. But really, I wanted to make up some lost time and finally tell you how I felt back then."

I swallow hard, his words settling much lower than my heart this time. Pressing my thighs together, I nod. "Okay."

One of his dark brows lifts as he drops his hand. "Okay?"

Lifting one shoulder, I confess, "*My* intentions tonight were to have a spontaneous orgasm, so I guess I can't be too mad."

His other eyebrow joins in rising into his hairline. "Spontaneous orgasm?"

A smile cracks along my mouth. "Eleni thinks they should be a little more..." I wave a hand around at nothing, searching for the words that don't make it seem as though my sister is slutting me out. "Impromptu. Natural."

Eli nods, returning to his food. "I see. So you intended to come here and get laid?"

I feel my face flush. "I mean... yeah?"

"Is it weird that makes me incredibly jealous?"

I bite into my bottom lip, unsuccessfully hiding my grin. "Is it weird I like that you're jealous?"

"I think it means I'm not a complete fool for still pining even after ten years."

Butterflies break free in my stomach, flapping around so frantically I think I might get gassy.

I've been out with plenty of men, liked some, and slept with a few. But there was never anything there that made me think I'd ever miss them if I never saw them again. There was no spark. Just awkward conversations that have to be had to make sure the other isn't some total creep and then a usual mutual understanding. Are we doing this again or looking for something better?

It was almost always the latter, and I never cared.

Eli, though, was always a different story. Even when we

only considered ourselves passing acquaintances in the hall, or tutor and tutee, there was something there. Something deeper than I could form into real words. A connection that simply exists.

To know it wasn't just me that felt all that is both validating and bleak. So much wasted potential. But I definitely understand what he was saying earlier. He's a social butterfly who loves being around people and charming them with his wit. I'd rather not. So to be together would mean one of us is going to have to make some serious life changes.

Drastic compromises.

We'd only end up miserable.

It's true. It's almost an irrefutable fact. But why does the idea of our date ending with us right back in the same place sound so fucking depressing? Especially after what I know now.

The idea of tomorrow makes my chest tight, and a responding idea blossoms from the glum reality. If this is really just meant to be for tonight, I might as well do it with no regrets and do all the things I want—including stepping out of my comfort zone.

"Truth or dare?" I scoot next to him and lean back into the booth.

"Let me try dare this time." He chuckles, the challenge clear in his voice.

I smirk, grabbing his left hand and slowly dragging it down and under the table until it rests on my knee. His eyes nearly double in size, but he remains quiet when I speak. "I dare you to show me what I've been missing."

Eli

CHAPTER SEVEN

When I initially started the game, I had a clear goal in mind. I wanted Mia to know how much I cared about her in high school and how no one I've been with since has been able to fill the crack she left in me.

Did I subconsciously hope she would pick dare so I could see how much I affect her physically? Maybe.

Was there any part of me that thought I'd be dancing my fingers along the hem of her dress in the middle of a full restaurant at *her* request? Not even in my sweetest dreams.

"Here? You're serious?"

Mia's bright brown eyes stare up at me, arousal flooding through them as she nods once. "I am."

Her voice is breathy, and the sound travels straight into my cock, jerking it to life.

I distract myself from wanting to fuck her right here in this booth by using my free hand to pick up my fork and scoop some of the garlic mashed potatoes. "Are you sure?"

Asking for consent twice is always best practice, and including an alternative option just in case. "We can leave now and check into our room."

Her lips part, but she doesn't say anything. She also doesn't look behind me to check if anyone is watching.

I like that. It shows she trusts me to keep her from being in anyone's line of sight but my own. This is a huge step for her, and I don't plan on taking that lightly.

Mia takes a stuttered breath before releasing a little laugh. "If you're scared, just say that."

This gets a grunt from me. I'm scared, but it has nothing to do with making her come at this table. More like the possibility of turning a simple attraction into an addiction.

"I want to know you're sure because this has been brewing for a very long time, and I intend to take everything you're willing to give me. And I expect *you* to take everything I give."

Her bottom lip disappears between her teeth, a shiver running through her as my words settle. For over a decade, I've waited for this moment, and I won't make the same mistake again.

Even if I don't get to keep her.

The notion that we only have tonight tugs at my gut. Doing this is going to open a door I won't want to close, yet even knowing so, I refuse to change course. I'll risk the ache, just so long as I have her this once.

"I'm sure, Brooks."

"Alright," I huff, stopping my fingers' perusal of the top of her knee, and tilt my head. "May I?"

Her delicate throat bobs as she swallows. "Yes."

Never has there been a more beautiful word.

I slide my calloused hand beneath her skirt, the softness of her smooth skin and the silk of the fabric feeling like the perfect walk to paradise.

Mia tenses but spreads her thighs as I move up, gliding along her inner thigh until I reach the thin lace covering her cunt. The heat from her core envelops my finger as I move the fabric to the side. I hover at her entrance, my eyes gauging her face for her reaction.

Her gaze is locked on the half-eaten plate in front of her. Her chest is completely still, and for a moment, I wonder if she's breathing.

"Mia."

Her lids flutter. "Yes?"

"*Breathe,* love."

She does as told immediately, sucking in a lungful of air.

I give her another second to relax, but when I don't move, she lifts her hips, pushing her exposed center closer to my hand.

Again, I check in. Maybe because a minute part of me thinks this is some cruel dream. "I can switch to truth if you—"

Her eyes connect with mine, the fire raging in them enough to burn my fucking soul. "Eli, so help me, if you got me spread eagle in this restaurant and don't—"

I push inside her, effectively cutting her off. The faintest whimper leaves her, and the sound is a balm on the cut she left ten years ago when we parted ways at the diner.

Her cunt clenches around the two fingers I have knuckle-deep inside her tight channel while my palm presses into her swollen clit. She's *drenched.*

"This is all for me?" I ask playfully, curling my fingers in a petting motion.

Mia's head jerks in the best nod she can muster as both her hands grip the edge of the table.

"Hmm." I reach for my water, my movement slow and deliberate. "Is this what you wanted?"

She shudders out a breath. "I—*yes.*"

I take a sip, pushing her slit apart with my pinkie and index and sliding in and out with my middle and ring fingers. The feel of her around my digits has my blood coursing through me so fast, it's damn near uncomfortable. My cock swells, pressing into my slacks, forcing me to casually readjust.

"I believe it's your turn now."

Mia's knuckles turn white as I stroke her insides. "Eli—I can't."

I chuckle, picking up my fork and stabbing into my lamb. "I'll pick truth. Would you like me to explain the tutoring?"

She pushes out a weighted breath, her hips now rocking lightly to give her friction against the heel of my palm. "Yes."

"My greedy girl," I huff, a lazy smile stretching across my face as her lashes flutter. She is overwhelmed with both the feeling coursing through her and the environment. "Alright, but remember you promised you wouldn't get mad."

I curl my fingers, rubbing against a spot that makes Mia's head fall forward. She tries to speak, but I continue my assault on the spot, granting her a little of that friction she was just seeking.

Her need to focus on my words—on something she really wants—only makes her struggle sweeter. "Promise you won't get mad."

My fingers slow their pace enough for me to do a quick scan around us and to allow her a moment to breathe. When I glance back at her, she nods. "Promise."

"Alright." I smirk, returning to my tortuous pace. I drag my fingers out and then push them back in, curling them as I do. "Other than movies, you and I hadn't really talked too much, and finding a way in was hard. You were kind of a recluse, and any time I was finally able to ditch my team-mates and try to catch you before dismissal, you were always gone."

I absentmindedly swipe a drop of condensation from my glass and push into Mia a little harder. "Another student had asked Mr. Clorey about tutoring, and he suggested you. Of course, I needed to get to you first, so I asked you before the next period."

Mia's eyes flash to me, and somewhere beneath the utter ecstasy, I see the flare of irritation.

I hold up my free hand in faux surrender. "I know, I know. I paid a private tutor for the kid who was originally going to ask you. He passed."

Mia scoffs, but then I press my palm all the way down, and her weak attempt at anger fades. Her responding moan is barely above a whisper, but for me, it's deafening. It plays in my mind like a damn siren's call as I draw my fingers out and push back in.

I can't help but smile as she spreads her thighs more. "My turn. Truth or dare, Mia?"

Her eyes widen as much as her furrowed brow allows, but she manages a quiet, "Truth."

"Do you like being finger fucked under a table in a room full of people?" I incline my head slightly, lowering my voice. "Does it excite you that they might see? Or arouse you that they can't?"

She shakes her head, the words not quite able to come out as I move quicker. She's so close already. "I don't—I don't know."

A low chuckle vibrates my chest. "Let's figure out which it is, shall we?"

At the same moment I focus on Mia's clit, Veronika appears at the far end of the dining room, her vision set on our booth. I know I don't have much time before she walks over, but I know if I time it right, I could expose Mia to her truth.

My fingers curl inside her, twisting while I press down harder with my palm. She drops one hand to the booth while the other lightly curls into a fist she that pushes against her mouth. The force of my hand makes her whimper into her hand, the skin blooming white beneath her teeth.

I lean toward her, brushing my lips across her earlobe and lowering my voice. "You're doing so good, Mia. Can I tell you something before I have you come all over my hand?"

She attempts to speak, but after the word comes out indecipherable, she nods.

A smile stretches across my lips. "This belongs to me, tonight."

Mia's eyes flash to mine the moment her cunt starts to flutter, and Veronika sidles up to our table. "Alright, this is your room key for the evening."

She places a card in my free, outstretched hand while my hidden fingers continue to fuck Mia. She's so close now, her entire body is beginning to shake—tiny tremors running through her limbs—and her breath is becoming more erratic.

"Thank you, Veronika. I believe we're all set. Unless you wanted dessert?"

I glance over at Mia, who is all but hyperventilating. Her eyes widen as she looks at me and then at our server. I curl my fingers harder when her pussy clenches, and she shakes her head vehemently.

"I'm good," she squeaks.

The server's eyes narrow, and for the first time, she actually acknowledges Mia. She inspects her clearly distressed face before pursing her lips and smiling back at me.

I flick my fingers faster, moving so quickly that the muscles in my bicep start to flex. "I'm good as well."

"Alright, well, I'll be back in a—are you okay?" she snaps, her eyes flicking to Mia, who's currently at the precipice of her climax. Her thighs secure my hand in place while her cunt squeezes around my fingers.

Mia doesn't answer, and I know it's because she physically

can't. The thought only drives my blood faster. I've never been so fucking turned on in my life, and a warm bead of precum at the end of my cock reminds me that if we don't leave soon, I'm likely to come right here.

"She's got a bit of a headache," I lie, pushing my empty plate to the edge of the table. "We'll take the check now."

Veronika appears slightly annoyed with how my attention has never wavered from my date but nods, slipping a black book from her apron and setting it next to me. "I'll be back to close you out."

She's barely a foot away before Mia combusts, her orgasm ripping through her and threatening to cut off my fingers in the process.

Her hands fall forcefully to the table as she rides the wave, my fingers still moving and drawing out every pulse. Nails digging into the table, she tries to find a steady intake of air, but my constant movement doesn't let her.

"That's it, love. I want it all. Give it to me." I continue my pace until her body stops shaking and her pussy finishes throbbing.

Her breath shudders as she finally comes down, and I slip my hand from inside her. She winces, her eyelashes fluttering with a deep sigh. "Oh my god."

This makes me chuckle. "I don't think he was underneath the table just now."

I bring my hand up and don't bother fighting the temptation of waiting to see what she tastes like. A deep rumble of satisfaction radiates from my chest at her arousal. It has my mouth aching to be on her.

"*Eli.*" Her slightly embarrassed whisper hiss is cute, and I can't help but try to store it to memory. "That was..."

She trails off, swallowing roughly.

"I think my girl likes the risk of being caught," I say softly.

"I—I can't believe I just did that. I can't believe I *let* you do that. And in front of that server."

I raise a brow. "Did you not enjoy it?"

Her head whips back and forth. "Yes, I did. I just... I can't believe how *much* I liked it. Hell, I'm not even one for public displays of affection, let alone anything like *that.*"

"Would you like to go now?"

Mia's head snaps to me. "Absolutely. But I still have questions."

I drop my black AMEX on the table and smile. "And I still have things I need to do to you. Let's go."

Mia

CHAPTER EIGHT

I've clearly lost my fucking mind. Like completely.

Not only did Eli put his hands up my skirt in the middle of a very crowded restaurant, he finger fucked me until I came while the damn server was at our table. And he did it at *my* request.

Never in my life would I think I was capable of doing anything like that. I mean, I literally masturbate behind a locked door, in the dark, under the covers, in an empty house, for crying out loud. Yet this man had me ready to beg him for a release, not even thinking twice about the dozens of people around us.

Not only that, but I loved every damn second of it. So much that I'm vibrating from wanting to do it again.

It was sneaky and fun, and I felt...free. Free from the constant ropes that seem to coil around my middle the second I get in front of too many people. The heaviness and dread that comes with taking a risk wasn't there. It was only Eli and the overwhelming feeling of euphoria.

My heart hammers in my chest as he finishes paying for our meal, and we're directed to the elevators. With every step we take toward the shiny metal doors, all I can think about is how horribly he's about to fuck up all future men for me. How I know for a fact no one will ever compare.

And that scares the shit out of me.

He taps the elevator button and checks over the pamphlet our server gave us with the key. The room that opened up wasn't just any room; it was a honeymoon suite on the top floor.

While pre-spontaneous orgasm me might have felt a bit awkward, I'm now taking it as a direct sign from the universe that it wants all these subtle feelings and obvious connections to be explored, and I'm... excited.

A sound *bings* and the doors slide apart to reveal an empty cabin.

"Ladies first." He gestures for me to enter, a wicked smile curving his lips. It unleashes a flurry of wings in my stomach, and my blood moves a little quicker.

"Thank you, Mr. Brooks." I pass in front of him, careful to get close but not make contact with his body. A thrill shoots through me when his heavy steps follow close behind, a small *humph* filling the dark cabin.

I turn, watching him press the large number twelve before leaning against the wall. His sandy hair falls over his forehead, and a muscle in his jaw flexes as he stretches his neck. His gaze rakes over me, this time much slower than before.

A delicious shiver runs down my spine, settling deep in my core.

"My turn." His gray orbs snap to mine, locking me in place. "Truth or dare?"

"Oh, we're still playing?"

He shrugs noncommittedly. "Unless you'd like to stop."

I shake my head. I like this. There's something about playing a game to make sexual decisions that take the pressure off. Helps with the inevitable nerves. While it's true he makes me feel comfortable around other people, I'm still a little bit of a wreck around him.

With anything new or different, there comes the initial phase of not wanting to do or say something dumb to embarrass yourself. But the game has a way of taking that away and making this simply fun. "Truth."

He pushes from the elevator wall and takes the broad step needed to close the distance between us. Goose bumps sprout along my arms as he invades my space, those stormy eyes of his searching over my face, making my breath hitch. He moves a hand, trailing his index finger so lightly up my arm I almost think I'm imagining it.

Desire drops heavy in my core as his finger lifts, sweeping across my collarbone and under my chin so he can angle my face up to his. "Tell me, love. If I dropped to my knees right now, would you let me devour your cunt?"

My thighs squeeze together, and my chest caves in with a harsh breath. Why do I want to say yes so fucking bad? "I—I don't know."

Eli leans closer, his lips an inch away from mine. "Perhaps just your mouth, then."

His eyes flicker down before he presses the softest of kisses to my lips. A jolt of pleasure ripples through me at the contact. His mouth is somehow soft and firm, and the desire to feel it everywhere damn near consumes me.

Eli backs away slightly, his gaze reading mine briefly before he sees the clear need and does it again, this time lingering a second longer.

My breath quickens as he does it one more time, my muscles drawing tight with anticipation. I grip his waist, my head beginning to swim, and in the next moment, both of his hands clutch either side of my face.

His lips crush against mine, and the world melts away in his fire.

The kiss is no longer tentative but needy and desperate. I've never felt such passion, and my entire body caves, relying on him to keep me upright.

His erection digs into my thigh as he slides his tongue along my lips, demanding entry that I give him immediately.

I give him everything. I let him do exactly what he said and devour me fucking whole.

My hands slide up his sides and around his back, where my nails dig into the thick muscle to hold me steady.

He groans into my mouth, his hips pinning me against the elevator wall, showing me just how badly he's wanted me. *Wants* me.

I lean forward, pressing closer to him, frantic to erase even the smallest of space between us. The years of wanting to do this, to see for just one second what it's like to be the receiver of Eli's affection, engulf me.

His fingers slide up, threading into my hair as he tangles his tongue with mine. It's as though he's been waiting for this longer than I have, and even the possibility has my clit throbbing.

After what feels like only thirty seconds, the elevator dings, signaling for us to finally separate.

Eli drops his hands, backing away slowly. I'm damn near panting, my chest rising and falling as if I've run a damn mile. But he isn't much different. His eyes are hooded, his breath quick.

"It's a shame we waited so long to do that." Eli smiles, but it almost feels like a sad one. Almost as if he realizes the same thing I do. We'll never get that time back. The potential. And giving in now will only make that regret so much worse because it's just for tonight. "Shall we?"

57

I nod, worrying my bottom lip. "We shall."

We step into the long, dim hall. It's a double-wide corridor with marble floors, chandeliers every few yards, and abstract art along the wainscot walls. He stops at the first door on the right.

Cupid's Peak is notorious for pretty much every aspect of the hotel. From the great slopes to the fine dining and the incredible service. But my favorite part was the rooms. They are essentially luxury studio apartments with a full-size kitchen, living room, dining area, and beds that I swear are bigger than California kings.

When Eli taps the key and opens our door, however, I realize I hadn't seen the nicest the resort had to offer.

Our hotel room has a foyer with a vaulted ceiling and a large chandelier. Rose petals line the walkway leading into the main area. Like the others, it hosts all the full amenities, except the bed is surrounded by a large white canopy, and decorated with over a dozen red roses.

The drapes are probably for added privacy, as on the far side of the room, the wall is made up of more floor-to-ceiling windows that overlook the resort. Directly next to the bed are two massive glass doors that lead onto a balcony. Eli steps in front of me, walking directly toward it.

He taps the light switch, illuminating the terrace and the round hot tub in the middle. The snow is still coming down, but from the looks of the downward trek, the wind has died off, leaving nothing but a beautiful view.

Eli turns slightly, his eyes finding mine over his shoulder. "Not scared of heights, are you, love?"

Mia

CHAPTER NINE

Eli gets the hot tub up and simmering with just a few taps on a tablet on the wall.

Still a little awestruck and maybe a tad overwhelmed by the room, a nervous laugh bubbles out of me. "I don't have a suit."

"Oh, but isn't that the best one to have?" He flashes me a lopsided grin that does wicked things to my libido. Hell, everything this man does is a deadly dose of an aphrodisiac.

Tell me, love. If I dropped to my knees right now, would you let me devour your cunt?

The memory of that moment sweeps in as Eli turns back to the doors. Crazy thing about it, my answer was so close to a yes it scared me. Genuinely. It's been well established the type of person I am, and nothing will truly change that. But in these small instances with him, when my head is all but delirious and my pussy is damn near aching, nothing else seems to matter.

Not his status, my shyness, our surroundings, or *our* end. It's like being in the eye of a tornado. While all those things swirl around, threatening to consume me, I'm safe in the middle with Eli.

It was something I've always felt, even in high school, but

could never articulate. Now, after years apart and experiencing it again, I can attest to the analogy.

My gaze flashes to Eli's, who's leaning against the glass, his broad arms folded across his chest and legs crossed at the ankle. He's completely at ease, comfortable and confident in every sense of the word. Rather than the slight sting of jealousy I feel when looking at anyone who exudes the same energy, I feel... *incredibly* turned on.

"Is it your turn?" he asks, tilting his head to the side. One of his brows lifts, and when his jaw tics, I have to squeeze my thighs together.

"Yep." I clear my throat, standing from the chaise I sat on while Eli played with the Jacuzzi settings. "Which one are you going with?"

He blinks slowly, his eyes never leaving my face as his tongue peeks out and slides along the inside corner of his lips. "I'll go with dare."

"Naturally," I joke, taking a leisurely step toward him. My heart begins to pound harder the closer I get, but I mask the wave of nerves with a coy smile. "And let me guess, you'd like me to dare you to strip down and go out on the balcony?"

Eli *hmphs*, lifting one shoulder. "The world is yours, Mia. You tell me what you want, and I'll do it."

"Anything?" I muse.

He nods once, and for the first time tonight, his facial features become serious. "Anything."

My pulse flutters with the way the word rolls off his tongue and the million different meanings it could have behind it.

Tonight was supposed to be all about a spontaneous O and getting out of my comfort zone. While those things are definitely happening, the path has varied a lot. With him, I want to push past what I thought was possible. I want to do and say things I've never been comfortable doing with anyone else.

I want to look back at this night and have no regrets.

Without a second thought, I channel my inner Eleni and say the first wild thing that comes to mind, surprising even myself. "I dare you to make me come without touching me."

Eli's brows lift to his hairline as he lets my request sink in. When it does, he drags his teeth over his bottom lip. "But you're allowed to touch me, correct?"

I swallow hard. His voice has dropped an octave, seeping deep into my core with every spoken syllable. "Yes."

A smile breaks across his mouth. "Location?"

I nod behind him. "Jacuzzi."

"Perfect."

In the next blink, Eli begins to unbutton his dress shirt. His fingers move swiftly, effortlessly opening each one with the subtle flick of his thumb. I'm not sure if he means it to be sexy as sin, but my breath quickens with every inch of his chest he exposes.

When he gets to the bottom, he strips the fabric from each shoulder, dragging the shirt down his thick arms. His biceps are large, slightly defined, while his forearms are the perfect mix of smooth and veiny. My body thrums with the sudden desire to have them on every inch of me, and I immediately wish I'd thought of a different dare. One that would have his hands all over me instead of not.

His wide chest is temporarily hidden beneath a white undershirt before he crosses his arms and draws it up over his head. Then, not giving me a second to really admire him, he's undoing his belt and stripping from his dress pants, leaving only a black pair of briefs covering his massive bulge.

It's easy to see how he's able to completely rock other hockey players on the ice, and I think I actually start to salivate at the broad, muscled physique in front of me.

He smirks, turning slowly to give me the delicious view of

his defined back, and opens the door. As odd as it sounds, his ability to simply undress and become even more confident in the lack of clothing is hot.

Unfortunately, my ability to do the same as him is not as strong, and I rush to the en suite. Butterflies lash at my stomach as I strip down to my bra and panties. Examining the delicate black lace, I send a silent thank you to my sister who forced me to wear my best. Excitement and nerves meld together in my limbs, making me somehow both giddy and terrified as shit.

Am I about to get in a hot tub with Eli on the twelfth floor where anyone could simply look over and see us? Absolutely. Am I a-okay with the possibility? Again, a resounding yes.

Why is it okay? I have no fucking idea, but I'm about to ride the exhilarating rollercoaster until we're both sated and heart-broken it has to end.

I quickly secure a towel around me and return to the bedroom area. When I step out onto the terrace, the chill of the night air curls around me, making me shiver. My skin prickles, my nipples harden into peaks, and my muscles become rigid bands. I remind myself that it's some of those things you have to endure if you want the core memories of the greatest orgasms of your life.

"It's far less cold in here, love." Eli leans against the back of the round Jacuzzi, his arms propped on either side of the edge. Steam whirls around his face, which is slightly illuminated by the small lights inside the water.

Every time I think this man can't get sexier, he does, and at some point, I don't believe my blood pressure will be able to handle the influx of work.

"Is it?" I ask airily, forcing a relaxed step forward.

A corner of his lips tug down. "I suppose that's a matter of opinion. Only one way to find out, though."

I roll my eyes playfully.

The outside is encased in dark oak, running vertically up the sides, but the interior is that of a modern jet-styled hot tub. It's black, and the low light beneath the surface is a tepid blue. Behind it, rows of balconies from the other rooms line the back of the resort. Most of which are dark, but a few have couples occupying them.

Again, I'm putting myself in the direct line of sight where if anyone simply looked, they'd see me. The notion makes my heart beat a little faster, my core clench a little tighter, and, if I'm completely honest, makes me wetter.

What the hell is happening to me?

Shaking my head, I rid myself of the inevitable doubt that always finds its way into my mind when I think of doing something outside my comfort zone. This is happening, and I'm sure I'll find myself recalling this night a million times over when I'm back on my Friday schedule under my thick duvet.

Eli watches silently as I strip the towel from my body and lay it on a nearby chair. Normally, this is the part where I find myself wanting to cover the exposed flesh and distract him with some type of sarcasm. But with the way his eyes are soaking in every square inch of me, I can't help but stand a little straighter.

He clenches his jaw, and again I'm met with an expression I can't quite read. There's gravity to it. One that keeps me pinned in place. The restaurant was one thing, but this—this is crossing a line of no return. It's giving in to the incessant pull, even knowing nothing will come from it.

I shift on the balls of my feet, my arms finally finding their way around my stomach.

Eli shakes his head, pushing through the water and reaching over the side of the hot tub to grab one of my hands. "There's no way in hell I'm about to let you get in your head about tomorrow when we're still in today."

I swallow, hating how much I love his hand in mine. "But why ignore it? Tomorrow is coming."

"And a lot of people won't wake to see it. Live with me in this moment. Right now. The one we've waited on for ten fucking years."

But at least I'm not going to spend a single iota of my life wondering what-if about anything.

My sister's words ring loudly in my ear. If I stopped just because I was scared of the sadness I'll feel without him next week, I'll regret so much more.

A heavy sigh whooshes out of me as I force the trepidation back.

Fuck it.

If I'm going to have the night with this man, I'm about to do it all.

A soft smile breaks across my mouth as I use his hand as support while climbing inside. The warm water consumes my entire body as I sink into it, wrapping me in complete bliss against the frigid air.

Eli releases my hand, and we both push back, sitting on opposite sides, only the steam and a yard's worth of water between us. "So, let's talk about the dare."

Dare

CHAPTER TEN

Mia

"What about the dare?"

Eli smirks. "Well, considering I can't touch you, I'm curious as to how you'll accomplish your goal." He lifts his arms, replacing them back on the edge of the Jacuzzi and adjusting in his seat. "How would you like me?"

The double meaning in his words sends a shot of tingling desire straight into my clit. Why did I do this to myself? All I really want is him all over me, exploring every little curve and making me delirious with need.

Now, I have to wait.

My eyes flit over his posture. "Just how you are."

He nods. "Alright, and while I work on completing my dare, can I use my turn?"

My brows knit together. I won't look a gift horse in the mouth, and if it's possible, he uses my answer as a way to find a loophole in the whole "no touching" clause, I'm all for it.

Nodding, I stand, watching the influx of steam swirl between us as I take the few steps required until I'm standing between his wide-stretched thighs. "Sure."

Out of my periphery, I see his hands clutch the sides of the plastic. Like he's already struggling to keep from touching me.

That excites me, making me damn near giddy. At least this won't be hard on just me.

"Truth or—"

"Dare." It's said without an ounce of hesitation.

Eli huffs out a bout of laughter. "Alright then. I dare you to reach your climax within five minutes, or I take over."

Thank fuck.

"Ten." I arch an eyebrow.

"Eight."

"Why are you trying to rush me?" Using the moment of conversational distraction, I place my arms on either side of his neck, gripping the outer edge. I hoist myself up enough to straddle the outside of his thighs, pressing my pussy right on top of his cock.

With only the thin fabric of our underwear between us, his cock digs into my sensitive center, and the groan that vibrates out of him is enough to have me clenching around nothing. "Not even my best self-restraint can last that long with you."

"With me," I repeat, though my voice is so low I'm not even sure if he can hear me. My hips have started moving of their own accord, rotating at the perfect angle, so he hits my pulsing nerve.

"Yes," he hisses, straightening his spine. "You are quickly becoming a very dangerous thing for me, love."

"What do you mean?" I breathe, keeping my movements slow and deliberate. My nerves are tight, the slight friction just enough to take the edge off. A part of me can't believe I'm here, doing this with him, without a care in the world. But the other part understands that's exactly what Eli does—what he's always done with making me forget about everyone else in the room—and I'm finally reaping the benefits. I want to *keep* reaping those benefits.

"I mean exactly what I said. You, this fucking body..." He

trails off, and I notice his knuckles blooming white from his tight grasp. "Every second my hands aren't on you, every minute my mouth has to wait to taste you, it's torture, Mia."

My teeth sink into the inside of my cheek until I taste copper. His words are nothing short of a direct shock to my libido. "Fine. Eight minutes."

His eyes flicker over my face once before he leans back, tilting his face toward his phone that's lying idle on one of the chairs. "Hey, Siri. Set a timer for eight minutes."

"Eight minutes, counting down." The robotic voice informs me the clock has started ticking.

I lean forward and lightly run my lips across his. He tenses beneath me but stays still, allowing me to appreciate the softness of his mouth. There were so many times I wanted to do this and now, I'm adamant about committing every part of this to memory.

My tongue sweeps across the seam until he parts his lips, allowing me entry. When I dip inside, a guttural groan vibrates his chest and urges me on. I'm tentative at first, exploring his mouth at my leisure. But on my second pass, he moves, trying to kiss me back.

"Uh-uh," I tsk, grinning as I draw back. "No touching."

A nerve in his jaw pulses. "Tick tock."

In an attempt to be a smart-ass, I press down a little harder. But when his cock pushes against me, a moan slips free, my eyes fluttering closed with the jolt of pleasure. "Fuck."

He grumbles beneath me. "My sentiments exactly."

A smile curls my lips. Sex and reaching a climax have always been a linear journey for me. I was so worried about making sure I got there that I can confidently say I've never enjoyed the ride. Never taken a detour and explored all the ways I could get to my destination.

Right now, with Eli under me and a night full of promise,

all I want to do is take my time. I want to draw out every moment with him, pushing my body as far as it can before it explodes. Then do it all over again.

I switch between hovering and sitting, rotating my hips until my heart is thumping and my clit is pulsating.

A deep groan forces my eyes open, and in no way was I ready for the sight that is a sexually frustrated Eli Brooks.

His head is tilted back, his eyes directed to the patio cover above him. His hair is mussed as though he's tugged on it at least once. Sweat beads at his temples, sliding down a clenched jaw I'm sure could break metal.

"Eyes on me, Brooks." I smirk, drawing his chin down with my index and forefinger. "I need you to look at me when I come."

"Mia," he warns, his voice a deadly octave as his arms twist at his side, that tight grip starting to loosen. But he listens, his hooded gaze finding mine through the swirling steam. "Be careful what you wish for."

And just like that, the idea of going longer and forcing him to wait makes a new thrill shoot up my spine, tightening my core almost painfully.

I'm stuck between wanting to grind wildly to find the release I so desperately need and waiting to see him as wanton as I am. The combination of the cool air, the heat of the Jacuzzi, the fire of Eli's gaze, and the feel of him beneath me pushes me to choose the latter.

I lean closer, brushing my chest against his, crossing my arms at the wrists behind his head. Sinking my hand through his hair, I tug, loving the sharp breath he releases. I ghost my lips across his earlobe, stopping to run my tongue along the shell.

It's the most sensual thing I've ever done, and my nerves

and pussy are quivering in tandem, the pressure and need building to a vicious high.

For a second, I don't think I'll be able to last, but then the ring of an alarm splits the air.

"Time's up, pretty girl." He smirks, releasing the hot tub. "My turn."

Eli

Mia de la Cruz is going to be the death of me. I'm calling it now.

It was cute, the little attempt at trying to tease me, but I'm not in the mood for wasting precious time. Not a single second.

My hands dive into her hair, and I pull us together, fusing our mouths in a brutal kiss. I tell her everything with it. How bad I want her—how bad I've always wanted her—and how she now owns every fucking part of me.

I wasn't lying when I told her what I felt for her a long time ago, and now, I intend to prove it.

Releasing her mouth, I grip one hand on her waist and the other around the back of her neck. She lets out a shuddered breath, her eyes blinking rapidly. Even through the fabric of my briefs, I can feel her cunt clench, her thighs squeezing my sides. "I can't wait to see if every part of you tastes as sweet."

She drags her swollen lip through her teeth and shivers against me. "Only one way to find out."

I smirk, my eyes drifting down her, finding a barrier I no longer want between us. The lacy black bra that's been nothing but fucking torture for the last eight minutes. "This needs to go. Take it off."

She swallows as she follows my gaze to the only article of clothing she has on. When it registers what I'm asking, her eyes flash past me toward the occupied balconies behind me.

There are roughly a dozen couples scattered along the various terraces and only half of which can actually see us if they simply looked. And it's that fact, the *possibility* of being seen—of being watched—that I need to turn me on.

Well, perhaps *needed* is a better word because never in my life have I wanted someone more than I want my fucking girl. Eyes on us or not.

"Does it make you nervous, or turn you on?"

Her beautiful brown eyes widen, but something close to excitement passes through them. When she doesn't answer, I drop my hand from her neck to her back, hooking a finger around the clasp of her bra.

She jerks back, her hands falling to my shoulders, her perfect lips disappearing between her bright teeth. "I—I'm not sure."

A small grin lifts one side of my lips. "How did you feel at the restaurant?"

Her lips part, and after a quick sweep of her tongue that I watch closely, she mutters. "It turned me on. But I was also fully clothed."

This gets a chuckle from me. Her not minding the people in the restaurant inflicts a stupid amount of hope in my chest.

"Then it stays on," I tell her, but when I start to slide my hand away, she shakes her head.

"No." She drops back down on my length, gliding along my erection. "Take it off."

Say fucking less.

With a quick flip of my thumb, I have the back undone and nearly rip the bra from her shoulders. I only mean to toss it to the side, but the wind catches it at just the right second, flinging it over the railing.

Even on the very edge of waiting to fuck this woman in the Jacuzzi and her a few mere passes from an orgasm, we both laugh. The sounds that flow from her are equivalent to honey and my favorite song, and I swear to God, I would do a lot of shit to hear it every damn day.

In the next moment, I lean forward, catching the melody with my mouth. She moans into me, grinding her hips with every pass of my tongue. My blood rushes through me, my cock becoming painfully hard at the thought of sliding inside her.

My hands find the swell of her breasts, my fingers sliding up the smooth skin until I find tight nipples. I pluck at one, earning a hiss that quickly melts into a moan.

Mia's nails dig into my back as she breaks from my lips, her breath coming in pants as she drives against me harder.

"That's it. Don't stop," I spur her on, gripping either side of her hips and guiding her movements. "You're doing so fucking good."

At the same moment she begins to quake, voices echo from directly beneath us.

Mia's eyes widen, her moan sticking to her throat as her hips still. When the voices grow louder—clearer with them moving onto their terrace—she begins grinding again, only this time much faster. Her hands grip the Jacuzzi edge behind me, and her head falls back, exposing her naked body for me to admire.

The steam, illuminated blue by the light, coils around her curves, lighting up a path I'll trace with my tongue later.

Leaning forward, I capture the top of one of her breasts in my mouth, biting the soft flesh. "Look at me. I need to see my girl's pretty face when you fall apart for me again."

"*Eli.*" A little cry of pleasure falls from her mouth as she clenches tighter to me, sending sharp spikes of pain down my back. "I can't—I—"

"Let me have it, Mia." I shake my head, thrusting her harder against me, using every ounce of fucking power in my

71

system not to join her over the edge. Her body begins the tell-tale climb, quivering and tightening.

The voices shift right beneath us, their vague weather conversation clear from their spot. An idea sparks, and I grip Mia's sides. "Trust me?"

"Yes," she doesn't hesitate.

In one swift movement, I lift her off of me and shift her toward the other side of the jacuzzi, right next to the railing. Her knees hit the seating, tipping her ass up, just out of the water that now laps at her laced-covered cunt.

"Hold on," I growl the command, my dick testing my brief's elasticity, as I admire the curve of her ass.

I smooth a calloused hand over her smooth skin, loving the way she melts, arching forward to wrap her fingers over the black iron.

Hooking a digit through the lace on either side of her hips, I pause. "May I?"

"*Please*," she breathes.

I smirk, and proceed to roll the fabric down, slowly. She's already at the edge, her nerves are tight, anticipation and need making her writhe and shiver. When I finally have her beautiful pussy exposed, my mouth physically aches to have a taste of her. To run my tongue from her clit to her ass and eat every fucking part of her.

But then she whimpers, her knuckles becoming white as she shifts. "*Eli.*"

"Sorry, love. Just admiring the view."

Her brown irises flash fire over her shoulder, making me chuckle. I slide one hand up her soft back and press down to hold her still, while my other hand positions at her entrance.

My fingers tease her slit, running up and down, circling her swollen clit until she's shaking. Her moans increase just enough to be heard over the chatter, the knowledge that people can hear her no longer holding her back.

Her hips begin to move as she mewls, twisting in an attempt to have me inside her. Her desperation is now my favorite thing in the world. A melody made just for me.

"Naughty girl," I groan, finally allowing her relief by shoving my fingers inside her wet cunt.

She cries out, the intrusion both a surprise and a relief, before biting into the flesh of her bicep to quiet herself.

I can't help my chuckle as I fuck her again with my fingers, reaching around to play with the sensitive peaks on her breasts. Her cunt squeezes around me, her orgasm so close I know she's a mere few passes from falling apart.

The voices have hushed. Either from departing, or wanting to place the noises coming from above them.

I lean forward, nipping the shell of her ear. "Come for them, Mia. Let them know how good you're feeling."

On command, Mia's head falls forward as her orgasm cuts through her. Her silent scream is both torture and relief to my throbbing dick.

Ripple after ripple of shivers wash over her, and still, I somehow manage to keep myself from doing the same, the sight of her enough to do me in.

I could never get tired of seeing her like this, and the reality I might have to soon irks the fuck out of me.

Another shiver runs through her before she slumps. I wrap my arms around her and shift us back where we were, and her face finds the crook of my neck. She nuzzles in, the act so damn soft and pure, I can't help but run a hand through her hair and stroke her spine as she comes back to herself.

The feel of her in my arms like this, giving in and trusting me, makes something in me click into place. Makes me realize that this can be possible. Some changes will need to happen, some compromises too. But I want her. I need her.

I refuse to make the same mistake twice, and after tonight, there's no denying the truth.

This woman is mine.

And it's time she knows it.

Truth

CHAPTER ELEVEN

Mia

"I'm screwed, Eleni. Like, completely and thoroughly fucked."

I'm currently in an extremely soft robe, sitting cross-legged on the massive bed, idly playing with some of the random rose petals. The deep color is such a stark difference from the white bedding, it's somehow helping ease the trepidation that's worked its way in.

When we dried off and came inside, Eli insisted on showers, even though I wanted nothing more than to be fucked on the nearest surface. He claimed doing so could mess up my pH, so I can't fault him for that.

He's currently taking his, while I realized after mine that I had about a dozen missed calls and texts from my sister. I'd forgotten to tell her about being snowed in.

"Are you saying he fucked you thoroughly, or..." She trails off, the humor clear in her voice.

I pinch the bridge of my nose, pushing out a sigh. "Not yet. But when he does, how the hell am I going to go back to my regular life?"

She laughs. "You don't. You get a mold of his dick and use it for your scheduled weekly O's."

"I hate you."

"I know." She chuckles. "Why didn't you take a shower with him?"

My shoulders lift in a shrug, even though she can't see me. "Someone called our room, and he left. He told me to go ahead while he took care of something."

"That explains why he didn't get in with *you*, but it doesn't answer my question."

Because as much as I try to be an assertive go-getter like my sister, it doesn't always translate. Hell, it never translates. Not until tonight. I've done and said more in the past few hours than I have in any of my little situationships.

That fact makes me hopeful. Makes me want to try things I've never dreamed of doing before. But only for him.

Like telling him what I should have at the diner that night.

My heart squeezes in my chest. Two sides of me I didn't even know existed playing tug of war. Living the way I have has been contentment. Comfortable. Boring. Tonight is lighting a fuse I'd long forgotten after Eli and I went our separate ways. But maybe... maybe I could try. For him, it wouldn't even feel like work to take risks, but something fun. Something to be excited about.

As though my twin can hear my thoughts, she clears her throat. "Em, listen. I would never condone or encourage you to change yourself for a man. But if you're naturally learning things about yourself and enjoy them... well, maybe it's not a change *for him*, but for yourself. And I fully support sexual liberation."

This earns a bitter laugh. "Not only are sexual acts in public ironic for someone like me, it's also illegal. I'm not sure you can classify that as—"

"Think of it as the light version of exhibitionism. The idea of being caught or watched, but not actually having that happen. It's actually insanely hot."

My eyes widen. "That's a thing?"

"Yep." She yawns, clearly unfazed by my possible sexual discovery. "Makes sense you'd like it too. It's not straight up out in the open but in the shadows. It's a pretty good mix of you and Eli's personalities if you think about it."

I swallow her words, forcing myself to digest them with the other thoughts already twisting in my mind. The possibility.

"Oh, hey, look who's on TV. Flip to channel thirty-two."

My sister's voice snaps me from my self-created rabbit hole. I glance over at the nightstand and grab the remote, bringing the television to life and clicking on the buttons to get me to thirty-two.

The screen fills with Eli's gray eyes, and my breath hitches. He's being interviewed by a woman who's braved the ice where heavily padded men skate around her.

He's got an easy smile on his face, the same charismatic one that draws almost anybody in, and his hair is wet, falling over his forehead. My chest swells with pride and admiration.

I've always enjoyed watching him and cheering him on. I never fail to wince when he slams into another player or gets frustrated after a fight and has to sit in the penalty box. It'll be harder to watch him after this. Knowing I had him twice and let him slip through my fingers.

Then don't.

My teeth sink into my bottom lip with the thought. Sure, I could tell him how I feel, what I want. But it doesn't mean he wants the same.

Just then, the interviewer laughs and asks if it's okay if she does his signature move. I'm confused at first because I've watched him for years and never seen a *move*.

Eli smiles politely, but it's clear from the way it doesn't reach his eyes that he doesn't want to. "Yeah, sure."

She lifts her index finger and pushes it slightly toward him, angled up. My breath catches in my throat as I watch Eli's ungloved hand reciprocate the move, touching the pad of his finger to hers.

I guess because I've always seen him do it with the bulk of the glove, I never realized, never put two and two together.

"Let me call you back, Eleni."

"Or don't," she jokes. "Go fuck that man till you can't walk right."

I flip off the TV, and we hang up the moment the water from the bathroom shuts off. My stomach tightens as I wait for him to come out, and luckily, I don't have to wait long.

Eli appears on the threshold, the same resort robe covering his frame. Droplets of water cling to his hair, sending a strange tickle through my hand with the need to push it back.

"Miss me?"

The question catches me off guard, and I can't help but smile. "Sure did, Mr. Bueller."

He smiles at my reference before taking broad steps to close the distance. But instead of coming to the bed, he goes toward the window closest to the bed. His fingers wrap around the edge of the curtain. "Open or closed?"

My clit throbs with the unspoken promise, and this time I don't even have to think of my answer. "Open."

A crooked smile curls one side of his lips. "As you wish."

"I don't remember whose turn it is, but I'd like to go."

He tilts his head slightly as he comes back to me. He stops at the edge of the bed before leaning over, gently unwrapping my legs and dragging me to the end to meet him.

A giddy laugh leaves me, the butterflies once again taking flight.

"How about this," he starts, gripping either string of my robe and slowly pulling them apart. "You ask me all questions you like while I fuck you with my tongue."

Eli Of course, Mia sucks her bottom lip inside her mouth, biting down on something I should be. The act makes my already hardening dick twitch.

I finish unwrapping her robe, slowly peeling away the thick covering one side at a time.

Without the shadows from outside, I have an unobstructed view at all that makes Mia so fucking delicious. From her perfect breasts that still bear the slight tint of color from my bite to her wet cunt hiding between soft thighs.

Her light brown skin is slightly illuminated by the nearby lamp, highlighting her curves in a way that makes my pulse throb.

I drop to my knees as I await her answer, my hands kneading her flesh. "What do you say, love?"

"Yes. God, yes."

"There you go again." I smirk, pushing her knees apart. "Begging someone who isn't here. Let's fix that."

Without waiting, I close my mouth over her cunt, sucking her clit into my mouth. On instinct, she tries to close her legs, but I force them back open.

I refuse to be restricted for all the ways I want to worship her.

I glide my tongue through her slit, my voice slightly muffled. "Ask your questions."

A moan falls from her lips as she drops her head back onto the pillow. I'll never get tired of that sound. I'll never get tired of *making* her give me that sound.

"O—okay," she breathes, her chest moving up and down much faster now. "Do you do our finger-touch thing on the ice?"

The question catches me by surprise, almost making me pause my languid lick. On TV, it's always been hard to tell exactly what I'm doing, but I guess in the restaurant, it was more obvious.

I release one of her thighs and walk my hand across her skin until I can pull her wet lips apart. Her clit is already so engorged. So needy. I press a light kiss to it, loving how she twitches beneath me, sucking in a sharp intake of air.

"Yes, Mia," I answer. "I do."

"Why?"

"Because it feels right. It reminds me of you and how excited you would get when my answer was right. You made me feel... good."

She lets out a whimper when I return to her pussy, or maybe it's finally settling in how serious I've always been about her that has her squirming. Once sure she won't try to close her legs, I let go of her other thigh and slide two fingers inside of her.

"*Eli.*"

"Hmm. That's my girl. You got it now." I continue my assault, licking and twisting, kissing and curling. "Do you know how fucking good you taste? I could do this every day."

Her moans are flowing freely now, the climax drawing close. "You should."

I chuckle. "Say the word, and I will."

Other than a playful huff, she's quiet for a moment, only the sounds of her harsh breathing and the slickness of her cunt as I glide through it, filling the air.

Something eerily close to doubt slips through my patched-up cracks. When I open my mouth to lie and tell her I didn't mean to pressure her or anything, she lifts her hips, pressing her pussy onto my mouth.

"Tell me a secret, Eli. Something you want me to know." Her voice is barely above a whisper, and the intent in it is clear. There's a hint of vulnerability in it, and I grab on, hoping this is the moment we stop treading around the obvious.

I let my fingers do the work as I rise, thrusting in harder to keep her writhing against me. "The lobby called before we got in the shower. They said the storm had passed enough to allow people to leave and wanted to let me know. I let them know we wouldn't be leaving tonight. Maybe not even tomorrow."

Out of all the things I could have picked—could have confessed—I chose that one. Why? Maybe so she can see she's already made me a selfish prick who's decided I'm not letting her go so easily this time. Or perhaps it was a little less forward than telling her my biggest regret in life is not fighting for her sooner. Either way, it's important she gets the message.

"What—" She's cut off when I curl my fingers, hitting the spot that makes a tremor ripple through her.

"I want you, Mia," I explain. "And not just tonight."

Her cunt flutters around my fingers, prompting me to return my mouth to where she needs me most. But I wait, wanting to say one last thing. "My secret—my truth, Mia—is that you belong to me. Always have. Always will."

With that, I find her clit, sucking it into my mouth before clamping my teeth down just enough to ignite the explosion.

Her orgasm slams into her, seizing her muscles tight. Her thighs squeeze around my head, locking me in place, while her fingers thread in my hair, keeping me right where she needs me.

And I don't stop. I fuck her until she's spent, her breathing is labored, and my mouth is coated in her climax.

Mia's cries of pleasure ring out, overstimulation causing her to jerk beneath me. It's only then I finally relent, removing my fingers and mouth.

I press soft kisses along her sensitive inner thigh, whispering my praises. "You feel so good, love. I can't wait to feel you wrapped around my cock."

She moans, her head falling to the side and staring down at me with sated, glazed eyes. "Then don't wait."

I smirk, lifting to rest my elbows on the outside of her legs. Running a thumb under my lip, I tilt my head. "Don't you have anything else to ask? Anything to say about my confession?"

Mia's head shakes slightly. "No."

"Can I ask you one last question?" I reach for my pants next to her, sliding the condom from my wallet.

"Of course."

I roll the rubber down my length before I stand, lining myself up with her entrance. "If I asked you to take a chance on us, would you?"

She smiles, her brown irises saying it before she does. "Yes."

That single word injects into my bloodstream like poison, corrupting my thoughts and making me believe the impossible is no longer unobtainable.

That's my fucking girl.

Unable to hold back any longer, I slam into her.

Mia

CHAPTER TWELVE

B y the time I realize Eli's going to split me in two, he already is. His cock fills me to the hilt, stretching me just past comfortable.

My hands fling to his hips, holding on as he draws out slowly. The delicious hint of pain morphs into pure bliss.

His heated gaze pins me in place as he thrusts back in, somehow pushing even deeper. My eyes roll back, the pleasure coiling low in my stomach before expanding out, unfurling through my limbs.

I knew he'd feel good. That he'd ruin every man after. But this?

The lingering euphoria from my last orgasm has my toes already curling tight, but it's what he asked me that has my body ready to repeat the climb.

He wants to give us a try. For there *not* to be any men after him.

At first, I'd have described tonight as though the sun and the moon have aligned, occupying the same space to create an eclipse. A rare event that only happens in certain parts of the world and only at the right angle.

To expect it to last would be impossible. Unrealistic.

But the more time I've spent stuck in Eli's gravitational

hold, the more I realize I've been thinking about us all wrong. How every morning, the moon can still be seen, even when the sun is halfway into the sky.

This could work—*we* could work—because even as complete opposites, we fit better than a puzzle made for each other. There is no jamming the pieces or shoving them past the slight resistance of the cardboard. We just... fit. Smooth and perfect.

"Holy shit, Mia," Eli groans through clenched teeth, and the noise drives straight into my core, making me shiver. "This was made for me."

He hooks both of his arms under my legs and yanks me to the very edge of the bed. Tilting my hips up slightly, he angles me in a way that allows him to hit a different spot. One that sends a sharp combination of lust and slight pain ricocheting down my limbs.

"Take off the robe, pretty girl," he commands, and the tone implies there's no room for discussion, not that I'd argue, anyway.

I'm quick to strip it off my arms and toss it beside me. Eli eyes it for a moment before deciding something and yanking the tie from its loops. He doesn't say anything but throws it around his neck, dragging his cock out of me, then driving back in.

My nerves sing with the sensation, a fire brewing lower and lower with every jerk of his hips. I've never come from penetration alone, but with the way he's moving, my libido hums from the possibility.

Eli wraps my legs around his waist before leaning forward, trailing his calloused hands over my skin, burning a path in the process. I squeeze my thighs around him tighter, trying not to let the need make me squirm.

"You feel so good, Eli."

"You feel better." He grins, giving an appreciative thrust. "Like you're mine."

My pussy quivers with the way that word falls from his mouth.

Mine.

His.

Fuck.

One set of his fingers plays at my collarbone, tracing lightly until he reaches my neck. The other hand stops its perusal under my breast. He cups the sensitive flesh and rolls his thumb over my nipple.

It hardens into a peak, sending waves of small shivers scattering through me. He's being overly gentle with me, moving slowly and only giving me barely-there touches. It's cute—sweet—but borderline torture. I need all of him, unrestrained and raw.

I trail a hand up, threading my fingers through him and squeezing my breast harder. A groan slips from his lips as I suck in a breath, moving our hands to repeat the act on the other side.

"I'm not a doll, Brooks. We've been waiting too long for you to hold back."

He releases a low chuckle. "I'd rather not scare you our first time."

"Scare me?" I maneuver his fingers to slide on either side of my nipple, then close them tight, reveling in the sharp prick of pleasure and the way his nostril flares. "Show me how bad you want me."

His eyes flash, and at that moment, I see a million scenes take place.

Visions of us on the kitchen counter, in the shower, on the couch, and over the balcony, all invade my mind. My insides ache with the desire to start and only stop when we can barely breathe. I want more of what I've never done before. More of that thrill.

"Take me there." I point to the window near the bed, my heart pounding harder in my chest. "I want you to fuck me against that."

"There? Are you sure?" A mix of surprise and intrigue stains his question.

I chew on my bottom lip, nodding slowly. "Positive."

"As you wish."

In the next second, Eli yanks both my hands down, crossing them at the wrist in front of my waist. He tugs the robe tie from around his neck and uses it to bind my hands, securing them together tight enough that when he's done, I can't move them at all.

"But first," he growls, pulling his cock out of me. "I want to talk about the diner ten years ago."

My brows furrow. I want to be confused, but my core is aching from his loss, the desire to have him inside me again too strong to focus.

A sharp pop rings through the air, and I cry out, a foreign pain sparking from my throbbing clit. "Did you just—"

Eli nods. "I did. You're not a doll, remember?"

He grips his cock and slaps it against my pussy again, this time with more force. I jerk forward, the overwhelming sensation sending shockwaves through my limbs. The pain is sharp at first, but it relieves the incessant itch. So much so, I want it to happen again, only faster. *Harder*.

Eli shakes his head and *tsks*, snatching my restraints and pulling them over my head. "Do you know how it felt when you let me walk out of that diner? When I thought I'd never fucking have you?"

A knot forms in my throat. I know how it felt for me. How hollow and heavy regret was. "No."

Another slap. This one feels even better.

"Do you know how many times I had to fuck my hand to the thought of you back then?"

His admission calls to the girl in me that did the same thing. The one that screamed into her pillow with his name on her lips.

I shake my head. "No."

Another. Now, my nerves are coiling tight.

"I wanted to show you right there. Bend you over that table and fucking brand myself on you so you'd finally get it. So you'd finally see me."

Subtle winks, crooked smiles, and brushed hands fill my memories. All the laughs in between math problems, all the trivia in the hall.

Eli jerks on my restraints. "Up."

He lifts me, holding my body an inch away from his. His cloudy gray eyes have shifted into raging storms, the fire he was holding back now free to consume me.

Anticipation floods my bloodstream, the promise and fear of what's coming next doing viciously delicious things to my imagination.

Eli leads me over to the window. At first, I think he's going to put my back against it, but he turns me around at the last second, pressing my naked frame against the cold glass.

Goose bumps flood my arms as he draws them above my head. Outside, the snow has started again, blocking most of my view, but I can still make out the soft glow of the other rooms.

I wonder if the other guests can see us. See my body, bare and wanton, squirming and wriggling under his tight hold.

Considering I can't see into anyone's room, I know the same can be said for ours. But the *possibility* sends my blood into a frenzy.

I turn to look at him in my periphery, watching as he strips from his robe with one hand before dropping it to the floor. He then grabs one side of my hips and yanks my ass backward, forcing me to arch my back.

"How fucking lucky would anyone be to see this sight." He runs the head of his cock against my soaked slit, and my eyes roll back.

"To see how gorgeous you are. Wet and craving my cock to fill you." His grip loosens just enough to let me thrust back, meeting his dick at the perfect angle to take the head.

A low laugh escapes him as he moves away from my entrance despite my whimper. Desire coats my every nerve, and a desperate ache blooms low in my stomach.

"You want them to see you, don't you, love? Want them to see you take every fucking inch of me?" He prods against my cunt, careful not to let my constant movement guide it in.

"You made me wait ten years for this, Mia. Ten fucking years."

"I know." My voice is a mere whimper, lost under the short jolts of pleasure as he continues to push against me.

"You knew I wanted you."

"I didn't—I wasn't sure."

Another laugh, only this one is much more menacing. "Oh, you knew how bad I wanted you. I all but fucking begged."

Eli presses the head inside, and I lurch back again, demanding more of it.

"My greedy girl. That's not how this is going to work." He pulls his dick back out and whirls me around, his hand still firmly above me, holding my restraints. "It's your turn to beg."

My breath shudders as I give in immediately. He hasn't been the only one who waited. The only one with regrets. Being with Eli will mean many things, but never again will I live with what-ifs.

"*Please*, Eli."

A brow lifts. "Please, what, love?"

I adjust under his grip, squeezing my thighs together to alleviate some of the pressure. "Please fuck me. I need it." I pause, swallowing hard as I give him yet another truth. "I need you."

He smirks, something soft passing over his eyes. "I've *always* needed you."

Before I can respond to the words that make my insides feel like goo, he hoists me up, pushing my back to the glass, wrapping my legs around his waist, and hooking my arms around his neck.

"This is going to hurt," he whispers, nipping at my earlobe. "And you're going to fucking take it."

When I suck in a breath, he grips my hips in a bruising hold and thrusts inside, hitting a spot that drives me up the window.

He wasn't lying. The new position leaves me completely vulnerable and at his mercy, opening me up wider than I've ever been.

How it hurts but feels so fucking good, I'll never know, but after a few times of him lifting and slamming back down, I get the rhythm, using his shoulders as leverage to meet his every thrust.

We fuck each other against the window, both of our groans and heavy breaths filling the air. We're completely in tune with one another, every second of us connected feeling like an intricate dance only we know the moves too.

"That's my girl. Right there," he groans, leaning forward and nipping at my chin. Then at my neck and down to the top of my unmarked breast.

Everything in the room starts to blur, the snow, the lights, his words. All I can feel is the climb. The tight ball of pure pressure slowly starts to fizz and streak through my limbs.

"Fuck." Eli drives in deeper. "No wait has ever been more worth it."

My heart swells at his words, but I don't respond because he shifts his hand to the front of my throat, squeezing the sides slightly. "And every single part of you belongs to me now."

His pace becomes brutal with his declaration, causing tears to spring to my eyes. My nerves are on fire, the end so close it burns.

"Mia. Do me a favor, love."

"*Anything*," I moan, the tendrils of my orgasm starting to unfurl.

"Come."

The command is said at the perfect second and he knows it. It unleashes the blind fury of my climax and lets it tear me to complete shreds. Pulse after pulse, my entire body contracts, the sensation both overwhelming and never-ending, and Eli fucks me through it, chasing his own release while prolonging mine.

My body has never expended this much energy, and when his guttural groan finally signals his orgasm, I'm spent, collapsing fully into him.

He immediately unhooks my hands from his neck and draws out, the slight string of his withdrawal short-lived as he cradles me into his strong arms.

His face is hard, his gray eyes narrowed in concern, while beads of sweat roll down his temples. That jaw of his tics again as he examines my face. "Are you okay?"

"Perfect," I say, holding my finger in the air.

He grins but doesn't touch the pad of my index until he's got me safely on the bed. "Did I hurt you?"

"Truth?"

He huffs. "Always."

"I'm sore as hell. But in like five minutes, I'm going to want to do it again."

This time, a scoff accompanies his smile. He leans forward

and presses a soft kiss to my flushed forehead, then my nose, and finally my lips. "What am I going to do with you?"

A dozen different things spring into my head with his question, but I tell him the idea that stands out the most. The one I always thought I hated but really secretly wanted.

"I'd like for you to stand outside my window with a boombox. Then I want a confession of your undying obsession with me and how you can't live without me."

I consider stopping there, but Eli's growing smile pushes me to finish. "After that, Eli Brooks, I want you to keep me."

"The Diane to my Lloyd."

This instant awareness of the infamous movie only cements how we're endgame. How we were always meant to be endgame. We just needed our third-act breakup like any great Hallmark movie, before finding our way back to one another.

He brushes a stray hair from my face before giving me a kiss that releases a dam full of butterflies into my stomach. When he stops, I'm all but breathless and ready to tell him I don't need the five minutes after all.

Turns out, neither does he.

Mia

EPILOGUE

W atching Eli on the ice through the screen of my TV and watching him in person are two *very* different experiences. I've been front row at all his games for nearly two seasons now, and I still don't think I'll ever get used to it.

The yelling is clearer, the hits are harder, and the fights are a lot more intense. Not to mention the pure energy that radiates through the stands, coursing through the thousands of fans.

When I first started coming, my social anxiety was at an all-time high. Even with my sister there occasionally, it was rough. But as soon as my gray-eyed man skated out onto the ice, it got easier. Soon, I became one of those fans who screamed and chanted, sometimes even wondering out loud how the referees didn't see the multitude of penalties.

Though, if I'm being completely honest, I still only whisper my complaints instead of actually yelling them. Even though they're wrong ninety percent of the time, I always feel bad for the different insults that are thrown their way.

Baby steps, though, right?

Tonight, I'm in the first row right up against the glass beside the tunnel where the players enter and exit the ice. It's one of those spots I both love and hate. At certain stadiums like the one I'm at tonight, it's on the side where the partition happens to be lower. And I could almost swear it's where the majority of the fights and hard hits happen. More than once, I've been front and center to Eli smashing someone against the sideboards or vice versa.

I do love that I can give him our touch when he passes me, though.

The massive jumbotron displays the remaining minute, and I cross my fingers that Eli makes it those few seconds without getting himself into any trouble.

And of course, because I think it, it happens. In an attempt to get the puck, Eli throws his stick to the side, blocking another player from advancing, resulting in a nearly instant whistle for a hooking penalty.

As expected, the whistle's blown, and a two-minute minor penalty is given. Eli does nothing but smirk, catching my eye and winking before he skates off toward the penalty box.

"Are you fucking kidding me?" one of Eli's teammates roars at a nearby referee.

I shake my head. Sometimes I swear Eli just likes getting in trouble. Well...

A vicious blush blooms over my face. Eli very much likes *almost* getting in trouble. Whether it be on a balcony, thirty thousand feet up in an airplane bathroom, during a drive-in movie, or even as a visitor during a crowded hockey game.

When the man wants me, he takes me, and I wouldn't have it any other way. Even if it means doing something really risky for a spontaneous O.

The buzzer finally sounds, releasing the players for the second intermission and for fans to take a break. As the boys skate toward the tunnel, Eli trails behind, waiting until I've scooched to the railing.

My pulse flutters as he nears, that same giddy feeling I always get lighting my insides up.

I lift my finger as normal, only instead of reaching his hand out, a sly smile lifts the edges of his lips.

Oh, gosh.

He reaches the railing and lifts, his eyes locked on my mouth. "Tell me not to, and I won't."

I lift a brow in challenge. "You better."

One of his heavily gloved hands cups one side of my face, and he draws me in, kissing me in front of the thousands of lingering fans.

My heart leaps into my throat, but unlike what it once was over a decade ago, it's in exhilaration. He was good about keeping me in the shadows while I made some life adjustments, but then he wanted me on his arm. He wanted the world to know that I'm his and he's mine.

I expected some hate and maybe even some jealousy and judgment that I was dating the player who was up for the Hart Memorial Trophy. But instead, I was extremely surprised by the number of articles that were released about us being the current it *couple* in hockey.

It was sort of cathartic reading through all of them and realizing that even though I've always been scared of judgment and ridicule, that's not always going to be what I'm met with.

Especially not with Eli Brooks standing at my side.

Left to wait for the end of the intermission, I scroll through social media. It's not something I ever used to do until me and Eli made an appearance together, but now I do it frequently to save any pictures we may have been captured in. Fans and journalists always seem to get the best ones.

Already, there's more than a few good pictures, fans, and two sports pages with the two of us mid-kiss, and all of them wondering the same thing; when he'll finally pop the question.

My cheeks grow warm with the speculations.

Ever since Eli and I took a chance last year, nothing was what we expected. We tried the long-distance thing at first, calling and texting frequently, video chats during movie night, and sending explicit pictures for sexy time. But we couldn't last a week without one of us flying out to see the other.

We made it two months before I packed up and moved in with him.

Thankfully, I work remotely, so it wasn't a big deal with my company. Being away from my sister, however, was a whole different issue.

Luckily, we came up with a solution fairly quickly.

Eli and I spend five months at home during the off-season and the rest wherever his schedule takes us. It's gotten me out of the house and exploring so many places around me, and I'd be lying if I said I'm not proud of the changes being with him has brought me.

I continue to scroll on social media, when a familiar beat plays in the background, making me sway. It's from one of my favorite movies made in '89—one of the best years, in my opinion.

"Love. I get so lost, sometimes," I sing the words, even though the song is challenging to hear over the ambient noise of the crowd. I've had it memorized since the first time I heard it, though. "Days pass and this emptiness fills my heart."

Ugh. Such a good movie. And that scene?

Perfection.

I nod my head to the beat, lost in a particularly good picture of Eli when someone beside me nudges my shoulder.

It's an older woman with long black hair, a huge smile on her face, and a pair of skates in her hand. She hasn't been sitting next to me this entire time, so I glance behind me just to make sure she's actually looking at me.

Though thoroughly confused, I don't want to be rude, so I smile back. "Those aren't mine."

She doesn't say anything and simply gestures to the ice with the tilt of her head.

Still baffled, I follow her gaze to the rink, where my mouth literally falls open, and my heart threatens to jump out of my esophagus. Sitting on the hood of a Zamboni is Eli with a fucking boom box above his head.

"You better hurry," the woman says, holding out the skates. "He paid me a lot for this, and he's only got a solid ten minutes before my cleaner is in the area he has to stand in."

Her words take a second to register, and when my eyes flit to the manager badge on her shirt, I realize she's in charge of taking care of the rink.

My gaze flashes back to Eli who is moving toward me at an incredibly slow speed. But the closer he gets, and the louder the song becomes, I'm running out of time.

Time for what? Well... I guess I'm about to see.

I hurry and lace the skates up, both eager and scared as hell as to what I'm about to skate into.

My nerves vibrate as I maneuver toward the small door that the woman opens, and when my feet touch the ice, the entire stadium turns to watch me, screams filling the arena.

A tight band of trepidation wraps around my middle, and for a second, I think there's no way I'll be able to move from my spot. I mean, as much as I've grown to not be as bothered by public attention, I don't think I've come *this* far. This is close to twenty thousand people we're talking about.

But of course, the moment Eli's gray eyes find me, nothing else matters. Only him and getting closer so I can be inside our bubble.

He sets the boombox down behind him and to my distress, jumps down, landing to the right on an uncleaned strip of ice.

The song continues as Eli skates to me, his hand out for me to grab. The last three months, he's been giving me quite a few skating lessons, and now, it all makes sense.

My lip disappears between my teeth as I follow him just off-center to the right. He slows to a stop before turning and grabbing both my hands in his.

"Let's play a quick game. I'll let you go first." His voice echoes with his words, and I realize he has a microphone on. *A microphone.*

"Eli." My eyes widen, but I keep my focus on him so I distract myself from the dozens of cameras flashing and yelps of encouragement from the crowd. "Are you serious right now?"

He gives me his classic smile, and even though I know he's exhausted, his gaze is nothing but excited. "Dead serious."

Tears spring to my eyes, burning the delicate edges as they cloud my sight. "Alright. Truth."

"Mia de la Cruz, I have been in love with you since my freshman year of high school."

I suck in a shuddered breath, and a lone tear spills over the edge, but I don't bother wiping it away. Not when there's a zillion more on the way.

"When we were in that booth, and you were teaching me how to pass Mr. Clorey's class, all that really happened was I fell farther down a hole. From your genuine encouragement, that addicting smile, and your laugh? *Ha.* Nothing and no one would ever be able to get me out of the hold you had on my heart."

"When life took us down different paths, there was a void left in your place, and it wasn't until almost two years ago that it was filled. When I saw you again and knew without a shadow of a doubt that we were made for each other, in each big and minute facet. I'm insanely fucking in love with you, Mia, and I have one question."

My hands shake as Eli releases me and kneels down on the ice. The Zamboni laps us, and the crowds erupt, shaking the entire stadium. It's funny how when I watched movies with scenes like this, I had to close my eyes or fast forward through them. But now that it's happening, I couldn't think of a better ending.

Another tear falls as Eli holds a hand up, and the passing driver of the Zamboni tosses him a small box.

He cracks it open and gives me his best-crooked smile. "Truth or dare?"

The End.

Ready for your next kinky holiday read? Pre-Order here.

Coming Mother's Day '23

Acknowledgments

Thank you, my reader, for filling your time with the stories in my head.

As always, thank you to my hubs who made this book possible with wrangling the kids and cooking me yummy meals. To my kids for always walking in when I'm writing the spiciest scenes. And to my incredible alphas and betas.

M.L., Felicity, Salma, Lily, Alexis, Lo, Erica, and Batool.

Y'all are the effing bomb and I hope you never leave me! Thank you for putting up with me being so last minute and needing everything done in one day. Like seriously. I love y'all.

CATTTTT. You came through. I can't thank you enough for creating such an incredible cover and blowing me away with your talent yet again. I'm so incredibly lucky to have you.

Kenzie. Where do I start? You pull me out the funk and bring my rambles to life. Thank you thank you thank you!!!

Eli and Rosa. The best out there! Thanks for always being down to read when I'm way past my deadline.

Again, thank you to everyone! I can't wait for the next holiday! If you paid close attention, I gave away one of the major tropes in this book!

About the Author

Lee Jacquot is a wild-haired bibliophile who writes romances with strong heroines that deserve a happy ever after. When Lee isn't writing or drowning herself in a good book, she laughs or yells at one of her husband's practical jokes.

Lee is addicted to cozy pajamas, family games nights, and making tents with her kids. She currently lives in Texas with her husband, and three littles. She lives off coffee and Dean Winchester.

Visit her on Instagram or TikTok to find out about upcoming releases and other fun things! @authorleejacquot

Made in the USA
Middletown, DE
25 May 2023